Wedding Bells

By JANET LAMBERT

Cover by Mary Horton

Published by Scholastic Book Services, a division of Scholastic Magazines, Inc., New York, N. Y.

For Elaine

Single copy price 45¢.
Quantity prices available on request.

1st printing................January 1966

Printed in the U.S.A.

CHAPTER 1

"HEY, BITSY, WHERE ARE YOU?" Vance Jordon stood on the back lawn and looked across the flower garden, hunting a younger sister who was always around when he didn't want her and invisible when he did.

"Here," Bitsy answered, snipping flowers and not raising her head.

She blended so beautifully into the mass of color that Vance had to peer over the rose hedge to find her. Her light curls, while not as golden as the chrysanthemums she was cutting, feathered out like their petals, and her cotton dress was the same dark green as their leaves. Even her eyes, when she looked up from between the rows, matched the blue of the late-blooming larkspur. She was color imprisoned in color, and Vance had to admit that she made a pretty picture.

"What's gone wrong now?" she asked, laying a long spray of white chrysanthemums on a newspaper beside a mass of yellow ones, and straightening up.

"It's almost time to go and get Anne. My gosh, I oughtn't to have to remind you of *that!*" Vance was disgusted. Anyone who could invite a schoolmate to spend the weekend—a super-attractive girl who was the absolute most and his present ideal—and then forget her, needed a valve tightened in her head. "It's darn near noon," he growled. "Anne doesn't want to spend her whole Saturday sitting around in that dumb girls' school, waiting for you. Want me to drive over by myself?"

"How?" Bitsy stood up and gleefully watched him prick his finger on a thorn. "It would be the trick of the week," she said, while he concentrated on squeezing out a drop of blood. "Susan went to the village in the car."

"Yow!"

The yell he gave couldn't have been caused by so small a wound so it must have come from annoyance. "Anne can get herself here on the bus," she went on, as if explaining sensibly to an eighteen-year-old baby. "I always go to Briarcliff and back that way, five days a week as a day student, so it won't hurt Anne to suffer, just once. She knows it. She'll be here."

Bitsy bent to move her newspaper heaped with bright blossoms, then straightened again. "I do wish you'd stop being such a baby," she snapped.

"Wipe off your finger and suck it. That's always first aid when you're pricked by a thorn. And please try to remember this—we're getting ready for a wedding here, and Susan has every right to take the car. It's her wedding."

"But not for a whole week yet. I don't see why we have to clean like crazy every day, and fill up the house with flowers. The groom hasn't even come."

"He's coming. Maybe today."

Bitsy Jordon was excited over the wedding. There had been four others in the family, but she had been either too young or too far away to enjoy them. She had been six when her oldest sister had married an English lord. And because she had always clung to Jenifer, accepting her in place of the dear mother who had died when Bitsy was a baby, she had been reluctantly taken to England to live with Jenifer and her husband, Cyril. Alice had married Jonathan Drayton from down in Bucks County, Pennsylvania, while she was away; Peter had married Tippy Parrish who lived just down the road from the Jordons; and long before, when Gwenn should have been gay and having dates, she had run off to marry a young movie actor.

Out of eight Jordons only three would be left now to have weddings: Neal, who was Susan's twin but only a third classman at West Point, would have at least three years to wait before he could support a wife; Vance, who was such a trial that Bitsy was sure no girl would ever want him, and Bitsy herself, just sixteen and with not a suitor in sight. This wedding seemed almost as exciting and wonderful to her as it did to the quiet Susan, and she intended to go right on filling the house with flowers and seeing that the next week ran smoothly.

Susan had had a frightful time making up her mind to marry the likable but irresponsible Robert Blaine Parrish, Bitsy remembered, snipping along with her thoughts and not caring how long Vance stood glaring at her from across the hedge like a grumpy old black bear. Susan had been just fifteen when Bobby had begun his stormy one-sided courtship, a truant from boarding school and a lonely little girl setting out on a pilgrimage to find a home for three children left behind by a major general who was far away in Japan. Bitsy had been safe in England, but she and Neal and Vance had felt abandoned. Tuition checks to a military academy and a girls' school hadn't made a home, so Susan, even then the staunchly loving, tenderly devoted little person she was today, had run away from school to hunt for one and had been taken in by Bobby's parents, dear, dear Colonel and Mrs. Parrish.

Of course, some of this new life had been Bobby's doing, Bitsy had to admit in all fairness, forgetting to cut as she mused about the past. Bobby had found the determined truant holed up with Alice and Jonathan, and it had been one of his crazy jokes to deliver her to his parents in their new house up on the Hudson, in New York.

His father was retired, his two sisters were married, so he had decided they needed another daughter at home. Ergo, Susan. That the Parrishes loved her was not his doing, but that he came rushing home from West Point for weekends to train her to be the wife he might sometime want was a well-planned campaign.

But he reckoned without the gentle Susan's dedication to an ideal. Once she had found this house—and it was a long time before Bobby could forgive his brother David's rich and beautiful wife for renting it to her—she had concentrated on collecting her family. Then her father had retired and come home to take a vice-presidency in a textile firm in New York. And I showed up a couple of years ago, Bitsy thought, sitting down on the path and being grateful to Susan. When I was so furious with Jenifer for having a baby of her own, Susan gave me a place to come to. "I doubt," she murmured aloud, a faint trace of British accent still clinging to her speech, "if I should have had the courage to be so horrid to Jenifer if Susan hadn't invited me to come home. I was a nasty, spoiled little snip when Susan got me, but I do think I've improved in two years."

"Want to go for Anne when the car comes back?" Vance called, having decided he had waited long enough for her to cut every decent flower in the garden; but she shook her head and watched him stomp off.

Stupid boy. Bitsy looked along the rows and rows of plants offering their beauty for Susan's wedding, then continued her musing. By twisting around she could look across the rolling acres of mowed lawn to a turreted mansion that rose against the sky even larger than Jenifer's castle. David and Carrol Parrish lived there. The vast pile of ivy-covered brick and stone was called Gladstone; and after David's wife had inherited it from her father they had made it into a beautiful year-round home for their three children. Bitsy always enjoyed walking up the steps to the wide, gracious terrace and having a real butler open the door for her. It was the way it had been when she had lived with Jenifer in England, and quite different from here in her own home where the sound of a doorbell would bring Irish Ellin marching through the house, wiping her hands on her apron, and muttering, "Sure and be patient, I'm coming."

Susan, however, preferred their own tall, white-stuccoed house with leaded casement windows and a tall round tower that held a circular wrought-iron stairway. It was called Gladstone Gates, because at one time it had been a caretaker's cottage. But that was long ago when Carrol's father had been living. Mr. Houghton had been a rich and lordly man; and it would surprise him no end, Bitsy reflected, to see the way David had turned the whole of Gladstone into a paying farm. She could understand why Susan loved the smaller house. She had been the one to find and rent it, and it had provided security and a happy existence for all the Jordons who had needed to squeeze in.

"It is lovely," Bitsy admitted, swinging back again to look at a smaller side terrace where summer furniture still invited a lazy hour outside, and on which, at the moment, a brown mongrel dog and a sleek black-and-white cat were napping. "It's a nice house. And if one is venturesome enough to climb all the way to the top of the tower, there's a faraway view of the tallest buildings in New York to the south, and straight ahead is the rolling countryside and a glimpse of the Hudson. I like it, but wouldn't want to be as mad about it as Susan is. Imagine! She wanted Bobby to build her one almost exactly like it."

She cut off one more stalk loaded with blossoms, then watched a car turn in between the two stone gateposts that marked the entrance to both Gladstone Gates and Gladstone.

"Hi," she called, snatching up her newspaper and squeezing through the gap in the rose hedge that Vance could have used had he had good sense. "Did you go to the post office?"

"Murder, yes!" Susan hopped out of the car and pointed to the back seat that was piled with packages. "Everybody who has ever known Daddy seems to have sent me a wedding gift. I'm terribly embarrassed."

She was taller than Bitsy, but anyone would know they were sisters. Susan, everyone said, was the beauty of the family. It had something to do with the wide set of her eyes and the sculptured planes of her face. She was as slender as a willow wand, and it had surprised Bitsy to come home from England and find her so, because her childish memory of Susan had been of a plump girl twin tagging after a sturdy boy one.

"I don't see why you should be embarrassed to take the loot," Bitsy said, shifting her flowers to one arm so Susan could stack a few of the boxes on the other. "We're always having to buy something for Dad to send to some buddy's children. Turn about's fair play, I say."

"But none of his buddies have so many children." Susan laughed, and with her own arms piled high, backed against the door to close it. "I have *some* friends," she said, leading the way along a flagstone path and up the steps to the terrace, "but that crazy Bobby seems to have collected them by the dozen from all over the country, and threatened them at the point of a gun. Has the great lieutenant been heard from yet?" she asked eagerly.

"No. His mother called and asked the same question." Bitsy managed to hook a finger under the latch of the screen door and to pull it open, but the dog and cat suddenly came to life and shot inside ahead of her. An astonished meow rent the air as she stumbled and dropped a package, and she said crossly, "It serves you right, Plush. Cassius, for goodness' sake, *move on!*" And pushing the box along with the toe of her brown loafer, she asked, "Susie, do you really think Bobby will show up today?"

"Who knows what that nut will do!"

Susan had always spoken disrespectfully of Bobby Parrish. It had begun years ago when he had teased her and lorded it over her, and had extended all through his last year at West Point and his three years of Army service. Bobby had been such a prankster that she had been afraid to take him seriously, and it was only during the preceding winter that she had been shocked into the realization that, beneath all his foolishness, Bobby Parrish really was as reliable as the "sturdy oak" he claimed to be.

"He'll be here when the Army lets him come," she said, and listened to Bitsy give a scream that made Plush's outraged meow sound like a whisper.

"Vance Jordon!" Bitsy shrieked, glaring across the enormous living room at a figure slouched comfortably in her father's favorite chair. "How can you just *sit* there and not help Susan? You're selfish and unfeeling. You haven't a drop of courtesy in you, and you're . . ."

"Aw, stop the flak." Vance locked his joints together and stood up to toss an apple core into the ashes in the fieldstone fireplace. "How was I to know Susan would come home looking like Santa Claus?" he defended. "Want I should take something?"

"No, not now." Susan cautiously side-stepped Cassius as she turned into the dining room and slid her boxes onto a long polished table. "Bobby gave me definite instructions," she said, coming back, "that not one single package is to be opened until he gets here—not even the ones from the girls I went to school with. If he doesn't come soon we'll run out of floor space."

"You through with the car?" Vance still had Anne Shelley on his mind. If he hurried he might still make the eight miles to Briarcliff before the delicate Anne had to set her dainty little shoe on the step of a bus. Weddings bored him anyway; and until Bobby got here to give a masculine touch to the whole silly affair he would entertain himself with Anne. But Bitsy flung her flowers and packages on the long sofa that now held the wounded Plush and snatched the car keys before Susan could toss them to him.

"I told you Anne is coming on the bus," she again reminded, wondering how she could pound the knowledge into his thick, selfish skull. "She wants to. She planned to. She isn't sure whether Miss Percival will let her come before or after lunch. So stop talking about it."

The Jordon children had had many arguments through the years. Gwenn had started an endless number of them before she ran off to her risky marriage, then peace had reigned for a time. Alcie never argued, Susan thought, listening to the two who were always ready to go into battle, because she was so sweet. Peter ranked next to Daddy after Jenifer married, and always went about in his quiet way; and Neal and I never fought. Vance *is* persistently annoying, so I can't blame Bitsy too much.

"Listen, both of you," she ordered, when it looked as if the key case would be wrenched from Bitsy by force. "Stop it! I thought you two had grown to be such good friends while Daddy and I were in the Orient last winter."

"Oh, we were." Bitsy flung the keys on the table and said disgustedly, "He was so scared when Daddy got sick over there that he was nice to me. And he stayed nice all spring because Daddy was still weak, and this summer because Neal was home from West Point and made him behave. But now he's being selfish and mean again because you're having a wedding and he can't run everything."

"Aw, dry up." Vance glared out at her from under a lock of black hair that always dropped down in a crisis, and swung up his hand to push the lock back.

He knew he was making a wider circular movement than the simple gesture required so wasn't surprised when Bitsy jumped back and shrieked, "There, you see? He tried to hit me!"

"No, he didn't." Susan wished Vance weren't such a throwback to the dark high-spirited great-grandfather he so closely resembled, and that Bitsy's maidenly feelings weren't so tender. They loved each other; and once in a while they showed it. But most of the time . . . Oh, dear, she thought, and was thankful to hear Ellin push open the swinging door between the dining room and kitchen.

"Lovey," Ellin said, smoothing back her gray

hair that was always fastened in a neat bun, and adjusting her bifocals on her button of a nose so she could see Susan through the top half of them, "the agincy tiliphoned while ye was away and said thiy'll sind us a girl to hilp out for the week."

"Good." Susan knew that Bitsy had hoped the agency would provide a butler like Perkins of Gladstone, and that Vance had wanted any man who had a strong back and was good at washing windows, but she asked, "Did they say when she can come?"

"This viry afternoon, if Vancey will go git hir."

"I don't want to," Vance began, thinking of the elaborate plans he had made to steal Anne away from Bitsy; but Ellin was going on:

"And the caterer tiliphoned too, to ask do ye want a three-tiered cake or a four."

"I stopped by there and ordered a four-tiered," Susan answered, nodding and with her mind already moving on to the next step in her busy week. "Will Daddy be home to lunch?"

"He'd better be!" Vance beat Ellin to answering that question, and hustled on to complain, "I don't see what good it did to buy the new station wagon. Dad hogs it for golf on Saturday, and he drives the old car to New York every day. I never get a shot at either one of them unless I have to run an errand for somebody."

"Cheer up, old buddy." Susan, on her way to pick up the litter on the sofa, patted the sleeve of his best sports jacket that he had put on for Anne's coming, and reminded, "Think how wonderful it will be after next week. I'll be gone and Bitsy can't drive."

"Nuts." Vance was not to be pacified. "Bitsy'll still be working in that darned old bookstore after school and I'll have to go get her," he argued. "It's better for me when you're here to do it."

"And for me too," Bitsy shot back, sure her grievance was far greater than his. "You're never on time, and I have to wait and wait, then telephone home and wait some more. Susan's always on time, and I'll miss her."

"Well, thank you both." They were ready to claw and bark again, exactly like Plush and Cassius fighting over a tidbit, and she said to stop them, "It's nice to know I'll be missed for something." And at that they threw themselves at her.

Vance scrubbed at the back of her powder-blue sweater until it parted from its matching skirt, and Bitsy left a sudden gush of tears on her gold necklace.

"Oh, Susan," Bitsy sobbed, "I don't want you to go away. I don't, Susan, I don't."

"Well, I'm not sure I want to go," Susan answered, a little frightened, as every bride is a week before her wedding, but keeping it light. "When my bridegroom gets himself separated from the Army and we can live in the beautiful house that Carrol and David are giving us for a wedding present it will be fine. But until then? Oooh."

She pretended to give an oversized shudder, but Bitsy knew that some of it was real. Susan had grown up with a deep fear of the Army because it could, and did, separate families. War she understood. Husbands and fathers must go away in wartime, civilians and servicemen alike. But peacetime moving about, so far from the ones you loved? She had fought against loving Bobby because she still remembered a child's lonely heart. And it wasn't until she had given in and agreed to marry him, Army career and all, that Bobby had told her he wanted to settle down, too, just as his brother David had, and become a businessman. It had all turned out as Susan had dreamed it: the new house under construction and a business financed by the family. And yet she shuddered. Bobby had received his education at West Point, so the War Department could refuse to release him until his three years of service were up. And for his last six months it could send him to some isolated spot where she couldn't go. What if it decided to punish him for dropping back to a reserve officer's status and sent him to Guam?

"I wouldn't worry, Susan," Bitsy said, sincere and eager to give comfort. "I don't think the Army will *want* to keep Bobby."

And that made Susan laugh. Even Vance's, "Sure, they'll be glad to let him out," provoked her mirth further. They were trying to reassure her, yet they were seeing Bobby Parrish as she had always seen him until last winter in Hong Kong, when he had magically appeared and taken over for her, and had brought her sick father safely home. No one could have managed tough General Jordon better than Bobby had. Not Peter, not someone who outranked the General, not even the Army's Chief of Staff. Bobby had been so masterful, and so calm and right. The whole frightening affair had shocked her into realizing how much she loved him.

"Well, whether he gets out or not," she said, freeing herself, "he's my man." And that made her laugh bubble out again. Bobby might never climb to such a dizzy height again. He probably wouldn't. But he'd be fun to live with, and a challenge. "I'll have to follow the idiot around and like it," she said, just as the telephone rang.

Vance made a dash for the hall, hoping to hear Anne's voice, but Susan pushed him away from the table at the foot of the circular stairway where the instrument of both good and bad news rested. "It's my wedding," she said, lifting the receiver, "so I'm entitled to take the calls. Hello?"

"Daffy-dilly?" came back. "It's me.

"Oh, *darling!*" Susan never got over the wonder of calling Bobby darling. For years she had hurled insults at him and had said, "Oh, darn it, it's you again," but now she repeated breathlessly, "Oh, hello, darling." But only silence answered her.

"Bobby?" she asked anxiously. "It is you, isn't it? You called me 'Daffy-dilly,' so it has to be. Bobby?"

"I fainted." The voice that replied was quavery.

"You were so glad to hear from me that I fainted from shock. I'm all right now."

"You nut."

The conversation was back to its normal idiotic banter, so Susan sat down on the bottom step of the stairway and prepared to enjoy it. "Where are you?" she asked.

"So near that I can fly across the fields to you. If I buckle on my fairy wings I can be there in four minutes, but if I wait for the garage mechanic to put some gas in my car . . ."

"Wait for the gas," Susan interrupted. "Your fairy wings were always flimsy, so wait for the gas. But tell him to hurry. Oh, Bobby, darling, *hurry!*"

Susan slammed down the receiver and swirled past Vance who was never above eavesdropping. "I see your precious Anne trudging along the driveway," she said, pointing through a glass panel beside the front door. "If you weren't always so interested in other people's affairs you'd have been out there to take her suitcase." And she danced out to tell Ellin that a real, live bridegroom would be lunching at Gladstone Gates.

CHAPTER 2

SUSAN AND BOBBY MET ON THE TERRACE, with Bobby shouting, "Hi, Bride!" and almost tumbling backward down the steps when Susan threw herself against him.

"Whoa there, Nellie," he said, swinging them both around to safety. "It's a long drop to down yonder. Let's stay up here and look at each other."

"Now why should we want to do that?" Susan meant the words to sound teasing, but she stepped back and surveyed him gravely.

Bobby's blue eyes still had the same bright twinkles in them and his firm full lips still had a puckish uptwist, but she saw them differently, now. Once his eyes had been only two dots she had glared into and his mouth only something she had wanted to slap—and might have, had he not always recognized her breaking point in time to say contritely, "I'm sorry, Daffy-dilly. I'll never heckle you again." He had, of course, as regularly as a clock's hands turn; and his parents, his brother, sisters, and even Trudy who was the Parrishes' old cook, had scolded him and called him a heckler.

"That child don't never give up," Trudy had said to Susan, during one of the times when Susan wasn't speaking to Bobby. "He can be mighty stubborn and mighty sweet, but he's a good boy."

The whole family agreed with Trudy on that, although his younger sister, Tippy, had always been reluctant to admit it. Tippy had been on the receiving end of too many of Bobby's pranks, so had stood staunchly with Susan against him.

"You'd be crazy to even *think* of marrying him," Tippy had declared only a year ago when Susan was visiting her and Peter at Fort Knox. "Any grown man who falls down and breaks his arm and then pretends that an armored tank ran over him—just to keep you here and turn my house into a hospital—doesn't deserve you. You shouldn't marry him if you *never* get married."

Susan had nodded solemnly at each impassioned word; but now, looking up at the happy face that had its chin on a level with her hairline, she wondered if Tippy knew how really wonderful and sweet Bobby could be.

"*Are* you a good boy?" she asked, remembering what Trudy had said and certain of his answer.

"I'm perfect. As Penny used to say, 'I'm practically perfect.'" His answer was glib but her question had surprised him. He had expected her to be worried about their communal future, to be solemn and troubled about his having to stay on in the Army after they were married and had taken a brief honeymoon, even to ask if he had enough leave for a honeymoon, or any money for it. He could have answered any and all of those questions, but he had decided not to, no matter how hard she coaxed. He wanted a perfect setting for his news: just the two of them alone in his car, and the car parked above the Hudson under a harvest moon.

"But I do have a worry," he admitted, kissing the tip of her straight little nose. "You're every bit as beautiful as I remembered you, but it doesn't keep me from having a teeny-weeny worry."

"Oh, not now!" Susan wailed, because she knew he wanted her to. "Not when I'm about to marry you and will have to share it. Oh, dear. What's bothering your teeny-weeny brain?"

"Me." He pulled her over to the old glider that had rocked Jordons of all ages for twenty years and said, holding tightly to her hand as if some giant monster might snatch him away unless she protected him, "What if I should turn into a solid citizen? I don't want to, but I might, and it scares me."

"Oh, *Bobby!*"

"I might, you know," he repeated. "Dad did,

and so did David. Have you ever considered how horrendous it would be for me if I should come to enjoy wrestling with monthly bills and changing diapers? I have, and it scares me."

"Well, it scares me, too." Susan sat up to glare at him in the old familiar way. "Five minutes," she scolded. "You've been here less than five minutes, and you've already warned me that I'll have to take care of the bills we haven't run up yet and the babies we don't have."

"Now, Susan, calm down."

"I asked you if you've been good," she went on, ducking his kiss, "and was about to ask if you're happy. But did you ask me? Did you care if I've been sitting here alone for three months, being completely and utterly faithful to you? Oh, no."

"I knew you had."

"Or wonder if I'd been sneaking in dates with Keith Drayton?"

"You didn't!" Bobby grabbed her shoulders then and glared ferociously at her. "Susan Jordon," he threatened, "if you've had dates with my ex-rival the wedding's off. I don't care if he is the brother of your brother-in-law and uses the family as an excuse to hang around. If you've been dating him I'm going straight back to Fort Knox."

"You can stay." Susan laughed and leaned against him. "Keith avoids me as if I have some dire disease, which I have—Bobbyitis. And anyway, Bitsy promptly took him over and his heart is mending nicely. I think," she teased, not in the least worried but wanting him to believe she was, "that the courtship of the Jordon girls is following a pattern. You couldn't get Alcie because she was in love with Jon so you settled for me. Now Bitsy . . ."

"Stop that!" Bobby sounded stern, but he grinned and gathered her close. "I was a silly little cadet when I thought I was in love with Alcie," he said, resting his cheek on her fragrant hair, "but now I've grown up. Well, I have," he argued, feeling her head move just enough for two mocking blue eyes to look up at him. "Didn't I have the good sense to get myself made aide to a flying general who took me to Japan in time to meet your ship when it docked?" he demanded. "And didn't I fly like a bird to Hong Kong when your father darn near died? Wasn't I the sturdy oak you've always been looking for?"

"Bobby, you were wonderful."

"Then what's all this about Keith? How did he get in our conversation?"

"Because I wanted to hear you say how much you love me."

Susan left him to figure that one out for himself. He might puzzle over it for days, twisting it around until he could come back with a smart answer. He might even wait to make a neat retaliation until they were walking back up the aisle together as Lieutenant and Mrs. Parrish, dissolving her icy numbness into laughter. So it surprised her to have him ask, "We were just teasing, weren't we?"

"Aren't we always?"

She straightened up to tell him more about the wedding plans, although she had kept him informed almost nightly over the telephone; but Anne Shelley, who had taken a quick peek from the side door at the newly arrived bridegroom, was already on her way to the kitchen to find Bitsy.

"They're fighting!" she cried, hanging over the counter where Bitsy was arranging her flowers. "They sat right down and began arguing. Do you think there'll be a wedding?"

"Of course." Bitsy stuck the last chrysanthemum in a vase and walked calmly across to an ell in the kitchen where a window looked out on the terrace. "Oh, pooh," she said, meeting Bobby's bland stare above Susan's head. And she raised the window to call, "Shall I bring you your lunch on a tray?"

"We're starving," Bobby called back. "If my future wife doesn't feed me any better than my fiancée does I'll waste away. Hustle it out, Bits."

"Coming up." Bitsy grinned as she opened the refrigerator door, and said cheerily to Anne, "It's going to be a lot more fun around here now that Bobby's come. He can stir up more confusion than a bulldozer, and you'll never know when he's serious and when he isn't. Even I don't, sometimes, but Susan seems to. How about unwrapping the sandwiches and putting them on two plates while I ladle out what's left of the salad?"

"Consider it done." Anne laid the halves of four sandwiches in neat triangles on two plates, watched Bitsy spoon out salad in unequal portions and transfer one of the sandwiches to the plate that had the Pikes Peak of mixed fruit on it, then rushed to the window and rested her arms on its sill. "Wow," she said, staring out. "He sure is good-looking!"

Behind her, Bitsy only grunted as she lifted a heavy silver tray from a high shelf, so she went on, "His face is thin but not too thin, and his hair is curly but not too curly, and he's tanned to just the right shade. No wonder Susan took him instead of Keith. I would."

Anne knew Keith Drayton from having visited Bitsy so often last winter while Susan and her father were in the Orient. Keith had come up from Princeton for news of Susan, lonesome and despairing at first, then, later, resigned and acceptant. She had watched Bitsy plump up his mashed spirits as if she were shaking a down pillow back into shape, so she waited for her to make a hot denial.

But Bitsy only said, "You can't compare them. Keith's steady, and Bobby's a nut. And if you're talking about looks, take your choice of blond or brunet. Keith's just as good-looking in his dark way as Bobby. They're both good-looking, so Susan chose the one she likes best, or loves—or something." Then she looked at the back of Anne's brown head and laughed. "Opposites attract," she said. "You've got dark eyes and dark hair, so naturally you'd fall for Bobby. Poor Vance."

"Poor Vance nothing." Anne whirled around and became very busy rearranging everything Bitsy had set on the tray. She ducked her head and tried so hard not to blush that Bitsy considerately turned back to the refrigerator again.

"We're ready," she said pouring one large glass of milk and one normal one. "When Vance gets back with the new maid Ellin will have her wash up after us. You might as well meet the groom now, since you're so melted over him."

"I am not."

Anne was thankful to have Bitsy's attention diverted from Vance's ardent pursuit of her and from her own slightly breathless pleasure in it, so she followed meekly to the terrace and watched Bitsy set the loaded tray on a low table before the swing.

"Welcome, almost-brother, dear," Bitsy said, standing on tiptoe for a kiss that touched her cheek lightly. "This is Anne Shelley."

"Hello, Anne. Susan has told me about you. Everything good." Bobby made a circle with his thumb and index finger, then looked wistfully down at the food his unfed system craved. In his haste to reach Susan he had driven all night, fortified by only a thermos of coffee, and now the very odor of ham and fruit unnerved him.

"I'll probably faint," he said, swaying so dangerously above the tray that Susan did what she was supposed to do. She pulled him down into the swing again.

"Eat," she ordered. "You can have most of my share. I'm not hungry."

"Is this all we have?" Bobby surveyed his heaped plate, the glasses of milk, the thick wedges of cake, and sighed. "Skimpy," he said, winking at Anne in such a friendly way that she felt like a conspirator. "When I have my own home Susan's going to cook all day. When she isn't washing and ironing she's going to slave over a hot stove."

"Taking everything out of cute little boxes and tins," Susan returned equably, "and popping them in the oven. And she's going to make a *terrific* effort to drive by and pick up the cakes and pies that Ellin and Trudy bake for her."

"In *Alaska?*" Bobby asked, stopping his half-eaten sandwich on its way to his mouth and staring at her above it. "Do you mean to tell me that you're going to drive all the way to New York from Alaska, just to pick up a pie?"

"No, sonny boy. From about half a mile beyond Gladstone Gates," she corrected. "From the three acres of land my daddy gave us for our beautiful house that's almost finished."

"But I'm ordered to *Alaska.*"

"Not this year." Susan grinned at him and said gleefully, "You gave your plans dead away a little while ago, friend."

"I did?" Bobby was so surprised and flustered that he forgot Bitsy and Anne, and even his lunch, as he asked, "When?"

"When you let it slip that the retirement board hadn't finished with you in time for you to start from Knox with Peter and Tippy, but that you didn't care. You even said, and I quote, 'It was better to stay and clear the paper work than to poke along behind a family with a baby.' End of quote."

"Well, shut my mouth." Bobby forked up salad; but when a swallow emptied the cavern behind his lips and Susan was still waiting, he said accusingly, "Tippy got here first and told you."

"No, she didn't." Susan looked up at the two who still stood awkwardly, with no invitation to sit down or an excuse to leave, so included them by saying lightly, "Bitsy knows that I haven't talked to Tippy. We don't even know if she's here yet, do we, Bitsy?"

"No." Bitsy shook her head and drew Anne in, too, by asking her, "Tippy didn't call while I was helping Ellin put out extra bedding, did she?"

"Uh-uh." Anne knew who Tippy was from having seen photographs of her wedding to Captain Peter Jordon, but she had never actually seen her or heard her voice. "Nobody telephoned," she said.

"There, you see?" Susan forgot her interested audience as she leaned over and took Bobby's face between her hands, stopping the rhythmic movement of his jaws while she said, "You gave it away all by yourself, and you let me know that you're as good as separated from your present career. You never could keep a secret, and you never will be able to. That's my only hope for our future being a success."

"Well, darn my ornery hide." Bobby looked glum. He looked glum but he also looked about for something or someone to save his pride. None of the three on the terrace seemed willing, there was nothing but landscape in the distance, and for once not even Cassius or Plush was around to provide diversion until he could squirm his way out of Susan's triumph, and could make her feel worried and uncertain until the moon came up. Then a long white station wagon pulled into the driveway.

"You didn't!" he yelped, endangering the tray with its glasses and plates by springing up. "You didn't go and buy a car before I own the agency! You wouldn't *do* that to me!"

"But we did." Susan laughed and looked up into his spluttering, outraged disbelief. "How were we to know," she reminded him, "that you'd be in business so soon? You didn't tell us you would. David didn't know, Mr. Whitlaw didn't know."

"He did, too. I wrote him." Bobby drew himself up and strode purposefully to the stone balustrade. "Good afternoon, General," he said pleasantly, extending his hand as General Jordon came up the steps. "Glad to see you looking so hale and healthy. Fine car you've got there."

"Thank you, son, we like it." General Jordon, wearing his baggy golf trousers and favorite old sweat shirt, paused. Once this cocky young kid, this son of his best friend and a nuisance to Susan, would have brought forth an "Oh, lord, boy, are you here again?" But now he laid his hand affectionately on Bobby's shoulder and said, "You'll get your commission, Bobby. I made that clear to Mr. Whitlaw because of what you did for me in the Orient. I owe you a lot."

"You gave me Susan, sir," Bobby answered. "You don't owe me a thing. Gosh, you overpaid me by getting sick and giving me my chance."

"That may be." General Jordon rubbed his thick shock of graying hair and looked about the little group with kindly gray eyes. "I—er—hur-rumph," he said, being prone to clear his throat in moments of embarrassment, "am glad—er—hur-rumph—that everything turned out so well for all of us. And now, if you'll all excuse me—I—er—it's nice to have you here, Anne—will go clean up."

He marched away, still a military man in his stride, and Bobby looked questioningly at Susan. "How could he mean that about my commission on his car?" he asked. "I don't even own the agency, yet."

"Oh, the deal's gone through, you dope," Susan answered, laughing. "David signed all the papers last week and kept Mr. Whitlaw on as manager until you're free. If you hadn't been so secretive and tried to deal with Mr. Whitlaw behind our backs, David would have told you. He thought you should suffer awhile. How were we to know," she said, spreading out her hands in a helpless gesture, "that Daddy—prudent, close-mouthed Daddy—would spill the beans?"

"Well, bully for the old boy!" Bobby shoved Bitsy and Anne against each other as he dragged Susan out from behind the coffee table. "I'm a man of means!" he shouted, upsetting a half-filled glass of milk that brought a shaggy brown dog up from nowhere. "I'm a businessman." And then, because he was a heckler and always would be, he had to add, "Or I will be in ten months. The board told me that after a nine-months' tour in Alaska I'll be free."

"Oh, Bobby, *no!*" Susan's eyes held the disappointed look he wanted to see, so he squashed her head down on his shoulder and said above it, "Go on, kids, beat it. When the hero surprises the leading lady with a beautiful ending to a corny play they should be alone on the stage. He's supposed to give her the good news and kiss her in peace."

CHAPTER 3

ANNE FOUND HERSELF ALL ALONE in the living room. Just fifteen minutes before Susan and Bobby had been unwrapping their wedding gifts in the dining room, Vance had been sprawled on the sofa with a plate of cake on his chest and Cassius licking crumbs from his face, and Bitsy had been curled up in a chair, finishing next Monday's English assignment. Then the telephone had rung three times.

The first call had made Bobby and Susan wade around an island of boxes on a tissue-paper sea, and go whisking off in Bobby's car. The second had put Vance on his feet, complaining grumpily, "Wouldn't you know it? I take one Saturday off from working at Gladstone and nobody can start the cantankerous power mower. I'll be right back." And away he had gone. Bitsy, the last to leave and not looking up when Anne went out to the hall to answer the telephone, had fussed even worse than Vance when Anne came back to say, "It's the mother of that new girl who came to help out—what's her name?"

"Donna. What does she want?"

"She said that Donna—but it sounded more like Dodda—has to see her lawyer this afternoon. She said that Dodda forgot all about it when she told you she would come today, but if she wants to get loose from that stinkin' guy she's married to she'd better hop down to the lawyer's office but quick. 'Just tell her, dearie, that I'll be right out to pick her up.'"

"Oh, darn it." Anne was an amusing mimic but Bitsy was annoyed. Donna was up in the attic helping Ellin unpack the dozens and dozens of plates that the kitchen cabinets wouldn't hold, the silver-plated salad forks and spoons, all the necessities for large-scale entertaining in the Army that had been packed away when war had scattered the family. "I'll go up and tell her," she grumbled, "but I'll have to stay and help Ellin, so don't be surprised if I don't come back."

So Anne was left alone. She liked the big room with its leaded casement windows and high, beamed ceiling, but she had seen it many times. She knew the pattern in the large Oriental rug, had stepped off the squares in the smaller one leading to the hall, and had sat in all the slip-covered chairs. So she decided to entertain herself by looking at the wedding presents Susan and Bobby had unwrapped, and was passing the French doors to the terrace when she looked out and saw a small procession cutting across the parkland from Gladstone.

A blond boy who looked like a young copy of Bobby came first. He was carrying something big that sparkled in the sunshine and might be an enormous silver bowl. A little girl with two stubby pigtails tied with red ribbons skipped along behind him, swinging hands with a brown gnome of a boy who kept trying to pull loose from her. And another boy of in-between size ended the parade, bent backward above a large cardboard carton.

Anne, glad for any entertainment, watched their progress and hoped they were coming here. The tall boy had a noticeable limp, and the little girl constantly stopped to pick clover leaves, her unwilling companion being forced to stop with her.

Now who could they be, Anne wondered, seeing that they were definitely headed for the Jordons' side door. David's children? Penny's? Jenifer wasn't here with hers, and Bitsy had said that Tippy's little Tippy Two was still just a baby. Then she watched the group divide. The two with the silver whatever-it-was and the carton turned across the garden toward the back door while the little girl and her prisoner mounted the side steps.

"Hoo-hoo," a high treble called. "Susan, dear? Bitsy? Are you home?"

"No, but I am." Anne swung half of the double screen door open and explained quickly, "I'm Anne Shelley, a schoolmate of Bitsy's. Nobody's here but me, so come in. They'll all be back."

"Thank you." The team started through, and Anne quickly held back the other half of screen so they could make it. "I'm Parrish MacDonald," the little girl said, "but I'm always called Parri. And this is my little brother Joshua, but we call him Joshu. Say how do you do, Joshu, and sit down."

For a moment it looked as if Joshu might mutiny and stamp his feet. Then he saw his captain's stern eye upon him and said obediently, "How do you do." And suddenly he exploded, all in one breath, "But I'm not a *little* brother. I'm nine years old."

"Eight and a half," his sister corrected, seating him in a chair by giving him a push, and choosing another comfortable one for herself. "I'm eleven," she went on when Anne was across from her on the sofa, "plus ten months and twenty-eight days. I'm sorry I won't be twelve by the time Susan's wedding happens. I'm to be her flower girl so I'd like to be twelve."

"Oh, yes, I understand." Anne knew who they were now. They belonged to Penny Parrish, the actress whom the world adored, and her equally famous husband who was a producer. "Oh, my," she said, just wanting to touch them, the way one kisses the hem of the Queen's royal robe. "It was nice of you to come over."

"We brought the punch bowl for the wedding," Parri went on, not impressed by Anne's breathless awe. She was accustomed to breathless awe, so she said, "Davy took it around to the back. He's sixteen, so he got to carry it. It wouldn't do to have a dent in it, you know, or to have the glasses broken. Lang carried the glasses because he's much sturdier than Davy is and didn't have polio when he was little. Davy's healthy now, though."

"I'm glad." Anne was about to ask if Davy and Lang belonged to David and Carrol Parrish, but her informant's attention was again focused on her brother whose wriggles warned her that he was about to squirm his way kitchenward, too.

"No, Joshu," Parri said, her stubby brown braids waggling emphatically. "You know perfectly well that Mummy expects us to behave nicely." Then she lifted the biggest, brownest eyes Anne had ever seen, and said, blinking the longest, thickest lashes, "It's difficult to be the children of a stage and screen star. We're so apt to get uppity. Either that or become delinquents. But the delinquent business only happens from lack of love, you know, so, fortunately, we aren't faced with it. Just the uppitiness. Are you the child of famous parents?" she asked formally.

"No." Anne thought of her mother who was in a sanitarium after a nervous breakdown, of her father who made a comfortable living as an attorney, and said, "I'm just normal."

"Thank your lucky stars. We have so much to contend with."

Parri ended her sentence with a sigh followed by silence, so Anne prodded, "What? Besides becoming uppity, I mean."

"Well . . ." Parri thought long enough to almost lose Joshu again. He was on the very edge of his cushion, one stubby shoe pointed toward the dining-room door when she suddenly said, ". . . Joshu and I have to be alone so much of the time. Of course," she added honestly, "we're always ready for bed before our mother leaves for the theatre, and after a play starts running smoothly our father always stays around until we're asleep. They're very considerate parents. However . . ."

"We don't get to go to school the way Davy and Lang do," Joshu put in, ready now to contribute something, and saying disgustedly, "we just have to stick around with each other."

"Oh, we do not!" Parri bounced her braids again and glared at him before she remembered that this was an unexpected social call with herself in command. "We do have to have a teacher who comes to the apartment in New York," she admitted, as if repeating her mother's explanation, "because sometimes we're there, and sometimes we're out here in the country, and sometimes we live in Hollywood. This year we're going to school out here because Mums isn't going to be in a play. You see," she said, turning to Anne, "our mother doesn't like being an actress."

"She doesn't?" Anne had heard that from Bitsy.

Bitsy had said that Penny Parrish, wonderful actress though she was, had left the stage after Parri and Joshu were born and had vowed she would never act again. Only her love for her husband had taken her back. She had stepped into the star part in a play he was producing to save it for him. Penny, Bitsy had said, was an absolute darling, but Anne waited to hear what Penny's amusing daughter would have to say on the subject.

"Mummy's an awful scaredy cat," Parri said proudly. "She grew up on Army posts where it was safe for her to run around all day and ride her bike, with Grandma and Grandpa always at home, so now she's scared to death that something awful will happen to us, like fire or being kidnaped, if she and Daddy are away. She's happiest, she says, staying out here in the country where she can wear old clothes and go over to Aunt Carrol's every day. Aunt Carrol," Parri explained, to clarify the family relationship, "was Mummy's best friend when they were young, so it's no wonder she saw so much of Uncle David that she fell in love with him and married him. She's very rich, you know."

"Yes, I've heard so."

Anne wondered whether she should prompt Parri again or wait for what might be spontaneously offered. Parri wasn't pretty, she thought, studying the little face between the big bows, but she probably would be when she could use lipstick on her large mobile mouth that quirked up at the corners, like Bobby's, and set her straight dark hair in pin curls. She would probably be a reasonable replica of her mother. Then Anne glanced at Joshu, sitting in a hump and resigned to waiting. Joshu never would be much to look at, she decided. Even at "eight and a half" he resembled a photograph Anne had seen of his father—dark, with a thin, craggy face and intelligent gray eyes. And she was thinking how fortunate it was that Parri had the better chances when she heard Parri talking again and had to say apologetically, "I'm sorry, honey. What did you say?"

Parri was chagrined to have lost her audience. Her mother never did. People sat in long rows listening to her mother, wishing they could stay there all night. "I was saying," she answered, changing her remark, since Anne hadn't heard it, and returning to a sure-fire subject, "that we live in a very close family group out here, with Grandma and Grandpa, and Aunt Carroll and Uncle David—and all the Jordons, of course, because Uncle General is Grandpa and Grandma's closest friend. We never go anywhere that everybody doesn't make a fuss over us, so we're always told beforehand that we're supposed to be seen and not heard. That's where the uppity part comes in. Trudy says we're uppity, and Mummy says we're practically hopeless. Everything is practically something or other with Mummy—practically perfect or practically awful—and she's always wanting to 'murder' herself or somebody. Sometimes she'll say, 'I could murder you for being so naughty,' or 'I could murder myself for being so stupid.'" Parri heard the kitchen door swing open and leaned forward to say hastily, "But not Mums or anybody else ever says that about Davy. He almost died of polio, you know."

"Uhhuh." Anne felt as if she knew the MacDonalds intimately now, so waited to see what the Parrish boys would contribute. Would they be extroverts like Parri, or the smart young snobs one so often finds in rich surroundings?

"Hi," David said, stopping in the living-room archway and letting his younger brother pass him. "You must be Anne. Susan came over to our house and said you were here. I'm David Parrish, and this is my brother Langdon."

"Hello." Anne thought David Parrish was about the most attractive boy she had ever met. She knew he was sixteen, but he made her feel young and as if she had been caught in the jam closet, because he said, "I suppose you've been getting this kid's chatter about us. She never misses. Is Bitsy around?"

"She's—she's up in the attic," Anne answered, provoked with herself for stammering. And she asked with great efficiency, "Is there anything I can tell her?"

"Nope. We unpacked the cups and Ellin'll know where to put them. Come on, gang."

He had the grayest eyes she had ever seen. The deep, deep gray kind that are like a cloud covering the sun. And he had bright light hair and square shoulders; and even if he limped a little she couldn't tell it while he was standing there. "I'll tell Bitsy you were here," she said, remembering to smile at Langdon, who was probably an average-looking boy with big hands and feet.

"I walked them over for the exercise so I'd better start them back. On your feet, boy," David said to Joshu, who was only too eager to part company with his chair. "Miss MacDonald?"

"I haven't finished my visit," Parri complained. "You promised we could stay awhile."

"You have. I'll bet you've hauled every skeleton out of its closet by now. March."

Parri stood up slowly, and her reluctant obedience made Anne wonder if Davy's father had handled Parri's mother in that high-handed manner. Bitsy had said the whole family adored David Parrish.

Miss Parrish MacDonald of the present generation seemed of a different mind, however. She simply smoothed out her starchy skirt, looked at Joshu who had leaped to his feet, and said, to test Davy's authority, "I think I'll stay awhile longer. Joshu, sit down."

"Uh-uh." Joshu had two stalwart males to protect him now, so he sauntered over to the door. "You're being uppity," he said, not crossly, only stating a fact. "Are you coming, or not?"

"Of course I'm coming. Mercy!" Parri placed the toe of one patent leather slipper slightly behind the heel of the other, courteously ready to genuflect, then stopped. "How old are you?" she asked.

"I'm sixteen."

"Then I don't have to curtsy to you. Goodness, I thought you were older."

"I'm *just* sixteen." Anne knew Davy was watching her, so she stood up, too, and said, "I do hope I'll meet you all again sometime."

"You will." Davy marshaled his brood out the door, Parri last and flouncing a little, and turned back to say, "I promised to deliver Aunt Penny's two by four o'clock, but you're going to be around for the wedding, aren't you?"

"I hope to come over from school again on Saturday morning."

"Then I'll see you. We've got big doings coming up for the whole weekend. So long."

Anne watched them straggle across the driveway toward Gladstone, where Davy took the lead and they walked as they had before. He seemed to have forgotten that he had them behind him until they were crossing the Gladstone driveway which curved around a small trim woods. One of them must have spoken to him then, because he stopped to unhook Joshu from Parri and send him back to walk beside Lang. So far as Anne could tell, watching through the window, nobody looked pleased with the change except Joshu, but she did see Davy grin before he turned around again and went on.

Anne was still at the window when she heard Bitsy run down the back stairway and push open the kitchen door. "Who brought the punch bowl?" Bitsy asked, wiping a smudge of dust from the front of her blouse.

"Davy Parrish and his younger brother, and the two MacDonalds. Why haven't you mentioned Davy oftener? I thought he was a little kid."

"He's only sixteen."

Bitsy took her loose-leaf notebook from the table and curled up on one end of the sofa, prepared to finish her theme, but Anne retorted, "So are we. Doesn't he go to the Academy with Vance?" she asked, following Bitsy across the room.

"Uhhuh, but he's almost two years younger than Vance and only a sophomore. His polio kept him back and I always think of him as terribly young. He's . . . ," Bitsy tapped her teeth with her pen, thoughtfully considering Davy, before she said, "I don't know what he is. He isn't shy or stuffy, really. He plays good golf and can jump a horse now, but he never seems to know when girls are around."

"He looked friendly enough to me." Anne sat down on an ottoman and crossed her arms on her knees. "He said he hoped to see me at the wedding, and he hinted that he'd have stayed longer today if it weren't for getting Parri and Joshu home on time."

"They're old enough to walk across the park alone. That's what I mean." Bitsy opened her notebook, then closed it again to say, "Don't go overboard for Davy, Anne. Aunt Marjorie says he's exactly like this father, and once Trudy, when she got in a talkative mood, told me that 'Mister David was the straightest thinkin' and walkin' boy ever was. There wasn't never anybody for him but Miss Carrol, and I reckon Davy's goin' to be exactly like him.' So I think . . ." She stopped suddenly because Anne had put both hands over her mouth and was laughing. "What's so funny?" she asked.

"Trudy's Southern drawl with a British accent," Anne replied through leftover giggles. "I wish you could have heard yourself."

"I did." Bitsy returned to her own clear, clipped enunciation and said sheepishly, "No one knows how hard I try not to use any British expressions. I almost said a whacking good game of golf just now, but caught myself. I didn't want to be an American when I came home from England," she said soberly, "because I was bitter and sure nobody liked me. But I'm trying awfully hard now, I really am."

"You're tops at school and loved at home," Anne complimented briskly, "but tell me more about Davy. Is he . . ."

She stopped because the screen door banged and Vance came in. He had caught her last few words, and without waiting for his faithful animal friends to follow, he let the door slam and asked, scowling, "Was that kid over here?"

"He brought the punch bowl." Bitsy gazed innocently at him and loved the way Anne fidgeted. "Four little people brought the punch bowl and glasses," she said, "and four little people went home. Heavens, but you're filthy."

"And the white side-walled Davy was dressed fit to kill, I suppose," Vance retorted. "Well, just remember this: He was making a social call while I was fixing his father's darned old mower. I'll bet he didn't mention that."

"He didn't mention anything to me," Bitsy informed him sweetly. "I was up in the attic with Ellin, so Anne entertained him. She's been dizzy ever since."

"Why, Bitsy Jordon, that's not so!" Anne hated her unfortunate habit of blushing, so she hopped off the ottoman and rushed over to pin Bitsy in the corner of the sofa while she cried, "I didn't talk with Davy but about one minute, and you know it! You're just trying to make me sound silly and boy crazy. I'm not. And I have a perfect right to know about your relatives."

"He's not a relative of ours." Bitsy thought of ducking under Anne's arms to escape, but Vance was only a few feet away and still scowling. He had a horrid way of putting out his foot when you passed him, making you trip and look awkward, so of necessity she gave in and said, "I'm sorry. Anne entertained that funny Parri the entire time and thinks she's a riot."

A car had stopped in the driveway; and since she was unable to see through a screen door that had a cat hanging on it and a dog standing on his hind legs against it, she tried to restore peace by asking, "Is that Donna coming back?"

"It's Susan." Vance decided to forget and forgive, too, and to show his sterling worth to Anne. A guy of eighteen, he told himself, didn't have to worry about a little kid, even a rich little kid. Just wait till basketball started. Team Captain Jordon would show her. He sighed unconsciously because basketball season was so far away, and said, "She's got Bobby's car. Maybe I'd better go out and ask her what she did with *him.*"

But Susan was already unpinning Plush from the screen and holding it open for Cassius to bound through. "Oh, golly," she said, coming in and putting Plush down, "Tippy and Peter look wonderful! And that darling baby. She looks just like Tippy. And she walked all around Aunt Marjorie's living room with her hands behind her back, saying, 'Mustn't touch.' I thought Peter was going to explode with pride. But do you know the only comment my lordly bridegroom made? '*That's* the kind of kid we're going to have. No nonsense out of it.' "

"Where is Bobby?" Bitsy asked, watching Vance move out of her path, so daring to get up.

"I made him stay home until I can go back and get him. After all, he hasn't even so much as said hello to his parents. Dad's over there, too, so Peter and Tippy won't come over here until after dinner. How's Ellin's assistant doing?"

"She isn't."

Bitsy explained about Donna's unexpected visit

to her lawyer, listened to Susan's vexed "Oh darn," then reluctantly headed kitchenward. "I'll go out and help Ellin," she offered, feeling as if she and Ellin had been partners the whole long afternoon. "Though I must say," she added, "it isn't very sporting of an agency to send us someone who couldn't last an hour."

"I'll go hunt her up." Vance was glad to leave this disorganized family that couldn't seem to function properly, and he said, "Come on, Anne, we'll go dig Donna out. You, too, Bitsy," he added as a courteous afterthought.

But Bitsy shook her head. "No, thanks," she said, feeling more virtuous than Vance because he would go riding around the countryside with Anne, presumably in line of duty but having a good time, while she would be left with the mess from lunch to clean up and his dog and cat to feed.

"Oh, go on," she said, looking like a martyr headed for the lions' pit. "I'll feed Cassius and Plush because you never remember them, but you can jolly well pick up all the paper in the dining room before you leave."

CHAPTER

4

"I NEVER SAW SUCH A DISPLAY!" Susan exclaimed, admiring the gifts that she and Bobby had arranged on tables along one whole side of the dining-room wall. "Why, we have enough here to start a store."

"Let's." Bobby looked, too, and said, "We'd make enough to feed ourselves for a couple of years and we wouldn't miss the stuff. Tin knives and dime-store china are good enough. Want I should put an ad in the paper?"

"Over my dead body." Susan leaned over to read a card laid inside a silver bowl and to check it with the list she had made of gifts and donors, and said with a sigh, "I have all these thank you notes to write before next Saturday. If I get behind I'll never catch up."

"I'll do some for you." Bobby was quite

pleased with himself for offering to be so helpful, but she shook her head and made a face at him.

"They're all *my* presents," she said, enjoying teasing him. "They're sent to the bride, so they're mine."

"Not the ones my friends meant especially for me," he contested. "Tony sent me that lacquered tray, and David said I could have our grandmother's silver tea service because he and Carrol don't need it. And those cigarette lighters are mine if I want 'em, and that big turkey platter and the matching plates are from the guys in my BOQ."

"But they all came to me," Susan retorted smugly. "I'm the bride, and all the loot belongs to the bride. It's custom."

"Hm." Bobby was silent while he looked thoughtfully at the laden tables, then his eyes lighted up with a naughty gleam in them as he said, "You sure have got yourself a mess of silver, haven't you?"

"Uhhuh. Candlesticks, platters, every kind of serving dish, flat silver, everything we'll need." Susan had forgotten their silly sparring, and she cried, "Oh, it will look lovely in our dining-room corner cupboards!"

"I wish you luck with the polishing of it."

"It won't take so long. On Saturday mornings we can . . ." Then she turned and grinned at him. "Beast," she said. And after she had spent several minutes kissing him, she added, "I'll give you half if you'll help me."

"Why, thanks." He liked kissing her better than sharing the wedding gifts, but Susan had removed her arms and notebook from around his neck and showed signs of going on with her work. "And could I please have a little spot in the house, too?" he asked plaintively, to keep her. "Just a small closet where I can hang my clothes, perhaps, or my own chair in the dining room, or one off in a corner of the living room somewhere? Just for me?"

"You nut." Susan didn't stay with him, but she did fling her notebook and pencil on the table to suggest, "Let's go look at our house. It has four walls, and windows and a roof, and we can take a flashlight. Let's not wait until morning."

"I'm scared of the dark." Bobby reached for her and stopped his foolishness as he held her close. "Oh, Daffy-dilly," he whispered, his cheek pressed into her hair, "you don't know how dark it was when I thought you'd never love me. There wasn't a glimmer of light anywhere, not in anything or anybody. I was truly afraid."

"I think I know. Sometimes," she said, her own cheek against the striped silk of the tie, "we bluff our way through shadows. You did a lot of bluffing, darling, just the way I whistled in the dark when I wanted a home and my family. I should have understood," she looked up to tease, "that you were whistling at a wife."

"Not just any wife—you. I really worked at it, Susan."

"Backward." Her soft giggle broke and splattered against his chest, and her arms that were creeping up around his neck again only stopped because Bitsy stood in the doorway.

"Could I see you for a minute, Susan?" Bitsy asked.

"Sure. Robert will get two flashlights out of the kitchen junk drawer while we're in a huddle, and will move Daddy's station wagon, so his car—I mean *our* car—can come out."

Susan could see that Bitsy was both embarrassed and worried about something, so she gave Bobby a quick kiss to send him on his way, then sat down in her father's chair at the head of the table. "Shoot," she said.

"It's about Keith," Bitsy began, still standing. "He telephoned and said he'd like to drive up in the morning, with Alcie and Jon."

"Well, why shouldn't he? He doesn't want to see me especially, does he?"

"He didn't say so."

"Then tell him to come." Susan was in a hurry to leave, since no domestic crisis needed her attention, but she took time to explain, "I'm going to Aunt Marjorie's and Uncle Dave's to lunch tomorrow, then over to Penny's for a family get-together and supper, but if you and Vance want to bother with Keith that's up to you. Alcie and Jon can come along with me."

"All right." Bitsy was unsure what one did to

entertain a discarded suitor. Keith had fitted in beautifully when Bobby hadn't been around; and he hadn't been gloomy and pursuing Susan, either. In fact, he had seemed quite happy with the younger crowd or enjoying the Jordons as a family. But now? "I told him he could come unless I called him back," she said, still hesitating. "What if Bobby has a fit?"

"Oh, he won't." Susan was already on her way out. Keith Drayton was merely a nice boy in her past, not too much in it, just a little, so she said over her shoulder, "If you want him, let him come." And out she flew.

"Of all the silly things!" she cried, when she had climbed into Bobby's long blue convertible and slammed the door. "Bitsy's in a tizzy because Keith's coming up tomorrow. Imagine!"

"What's he coming for?"

Bobby, in the glow from the dashboard and with moonlight playing on his face like a spotlight, looked as upset as Bitsy had. And before she could answer he demanded, "Did you tell her to *let* him?"

"Of course. He doesn't bother me. Let's get going."

"Well, he bothers me."

Their closeness had been shattered. Bobby's face was grim, and he looked unmovable. "This is *my* time," he said. "I'm supposed to enjoy it, and I can't with that clown around. Go in and tell Bitsy to phone him back that he can't come."

"Don't be silly." Susan thought he was still

teasing. There had been other girls in Bobby's life, dozens of them, and she wasn't jealous of them. They had come and gone before he belonged to her. His life, up to last winter, had been far apart from hers. So she said, "Drive on, man."

But he still sat, stiff and straight and not starting the motor. "No," he said, glaring straight ahead. "I don't intend to share my Sunday with Keith Drayton, or any days afterward." And then she knew he meant it.

For a flash of a second Susan was just as angry as he was. Her chin lifted and her shoulders drew back; then reason returned, and she said calmly, "Let's get something straight, Robert Blaine. I'm not quite twenty to your twenty-six, and I don't intend to be adult while you remain an adolescent. I'm not marrying you to mother you. I've told you that I love you. I want to be your wife and live with you forever and ever. Doesn't that prove anything to you?"

"Yes," he agreed reluctantly.

"Then how can you expect me," she asked reasonably, turning sidewise to face him, "to live here in a community where we'll be friends with the young crowd of married, or *unmarried*, girls that you used to date? How can we go to parties with them when you won't accept a boy who is almost a member of my family?"

"Those girls don't matter a whoop to me, now."

"But once they did." Susan's chin was smaller than his, but it was just as determined and high as she said, "Don't forget, my friend, that I remember the way you used to moon over Willa Levering and Dorothea Tyler, or that you sent me on my bicycle to pick up corsages for Kitty Ames. They won't bother me at all, because I like them, but you can't keep me a prisoner in my own home—afraid to go see my own sister because her brother-in-law might be there, or to have her family come to see me. If I marry you, Bobby, trust has to work both ways."

"What do you mean, 'if'?" He was frightened now; and wondering if he had gone too far in his possessiveness, he turned to coax her back to him. But her gaze met his, level and icy blue.

"Just what I said. We must come to a mutual understanding and some agreement if I'm to marry you."

"You mean, you might not?"

"I don't know."

She wrenched her eyes away from him and closed them against the sight of his dear face. A still small voice told her that now was the time to have a showdown with Bobby. After five o'clock next Saturday afternoon it would be too late. Her identity would be gone, her present and future with it, and she would be no more than Mrs. Robert Blaine Parrish, the target for Bobby's orders.

"I'm Susan Jordon, Bobby," she said. "If I were to add Parrish to my name I'd still have to be Susan. I love you, oh, so very dearly, and I trust you. But you'd have to trust me, too.

You don't, so I wouldn't have much of a life. Love can't be kept shut up inside four walls, Bobby."

"I wouldn't do that to you, Daffy-dilly."

"You're trying to."

Susan felt so calm that she wondered if she had any feelings at all. Her chest felt like a great flat plain, like the regions on the moon perhaps, waiting for signals to contact it, asking if there was any life there. She saw the dark shapes of trees, the two lanterns on the stone gateposts shining their welcome into the night, but she didn't feel her hand reaching for the chromium handle on the door. "I'm sorry," she said, looking straight ahead. "I'm sorry for us both."

"*Susan!*" Bobby snatched her hand and held it tightly in both of his. "I love you," he argued. "I want you. I don't want anyone else in the world. I was only kidding when I sounded off about Keith. Believe me, Susan."

But she shook her head. "No, you weren't," she said. "I thought you were this afternoon, but I should have known it was only your childish way of telling me that I must give in to you. Your love isn't deep enough, Bobby."

"But it is," he pleaded. "If you'll just give me a chance to show you how I can cherish you and make you happy—if you'll watch how good in business I'm going to be, and . . ."

"I don't want to watch you in business," Susan broke in. "That's exactly the point. I trust you. I don't want to stay home and sigh to myself,

'Bobby's selling a car to one of his old girls today,' and I don't want you telling yourself, 'Susan has driven down to Alcie's so she'll see Keith.' I couldn't live that way, Bobby, I couldn't be happy. Perhaps," she said carefully, "I'm too young for you—or else, too old."

"Darling." Bobby laid his arm across her shoulders and she let it rest there. "Please," he whispered, "I'll never mention Keith again as long as I live. I promise." There was no answer, so he dared again, "Let's go look at our house, Daffy-dilly. If we see our house in the moonlight, a sturdy fort for our love, everything will be all right. You'll forget how nasty I've been and will love me again."

"I love you now," Susan said. "I love you more than anything in the world, but that doesn't mean," she explained with a sigh, "that I can accept your possessiveness. I'm sorry, darling." She leaned close to him and he could see tears rolling slowly down her cheeks as she said, "I have to stay Susan, not Daffy-dilly or Mrs. Parrish. I'm only nineteen, but, somehow, I know I must always be Susan until I die. I can't argue any more, so good night, darling."

The car door was a long time opening behind her because she had to push his arms away while she fumbled for its handle, but at last she was on the flagstone path and running toward the lighted house.

She didn't know if her marriage was over before it began, but she did know that a house built of straw, or cards, or blind worship, could never stand through constant gales of jealousy. And stopping her flight in the upstairs hall, looking down through the tall window at a car still sitting in the driveway, she pitied Bobby even more than she pitied herself. "Please help us, God," she whispered, her face pressed against the cool upper half of the pane, "because I don't know what to do."

Bobby sat where she had left him. He wanted to run after her, to batter his way to wherever she was, to kiss her, convince her of a shared mutual trust, but he knew that Susan's words made sense. The quarrel, if one could call it a quarrel, had begun so suddenly and ended so quickly that it had left him dazed.

Lord knows, he wanted to spend the rest of his life with Susan, he told himself, making her happy and being a little happy himself, but he couldn't do it if she had to have that greedy character always hanging around. It looked as if she wanted them both: Keith to entertain her during the day, and a tired, pooped husband at the end of it. She was selfish, that's what she was. She wanted him, and Keith, and all the wedding presents.

His thoughts were somber, and the longer he sat waiting for Susan to come back and unsay all the crazy things she had said, the more convinced he became that he was quite apt to be as unmarried next Saturday night as he was now. Susan, like the Supreme Court, wasn't much on reversing a decision.

"Darn it," he growled.

One hand half-reached for the door as if deciding to open the way for his willing feet to carry him toward Susan, but the other one, his reliable right hand, flipped on the ignition. And his surprised, muddled mind came out of its fog to tell him that any guy who gave in to a girl on the question of another man, on the very eve of his wedding, was a pigeon.

"Okay," he said, feeling strong and self-righteous, "if that's the way you want it, Miss Jordon, it's the way you've got it." And with a spurt of gravel he headed the car at the gateway.

He didn't know where he was going. Certainly not home, where Susan's brother and father would glance at their watches and show surprise at his early return, where his own mother and father would question him anxiously, where Tippy would jump right into the middle of the mess and call him a heel. He was too miserable to think, so his car automatically turned itself left on the asphalt road, and he found himself headed for Penny's.

Lights were on in the old farmhouse that Penny and Josh had bought; and as he sat uncertainly in the driveway, wondering if he should go in to talk over his troubles, the front door opened and Penny looked out.

"Come on in, Bobby," she called, recognizing the rakish car that was exactly what her bachelor brother would buy. "Bring Susan and come in." Then she switched on the outside lamps and looked more closely. "Are you alone?" she asked.

"Yep." Bobby's decision had been made for him so he slid out and strode up the steps. "Just thought I'd drop by," he said pleasantly. "Susan went to bed and I didn't feel like going home to all the yakking. I'm not much on the family circle sort of stuff. Hi, how are you?"

"Fine. It's nice to have you back after three months," she said, giving him a kiss and a pat. She wore the yellow lounging pajamas he had brought her from Hong Kong, and her brown hair hung loosely about her shoulders, caught back from her face and held by a pink rose that Josh had fastened there. "Bobby's here, darling," she called, the stiff brocade making whispering noises as she led the way to the living room. "All by himself, at nine-thirty in the evening."

Bobby knew she was broadcasting in code to Josh, but he was past caring. The whole family would tear the quarrel to shreds tomorrow, anyway, each clutching a piece of it, so he watched Josh lay down the blue-jacketed play he had been reading and come toward him.

"Hi, fellow," Josh said in his kind way that always made Bobby feel as if he were the one person Josh wanted most to see at the moment. "It's good to know you're going to be our neighbor. Come on in. Penny and I have just decided to buy ourselves another play, after a whole evening of agonizing, so sit down and bring us back to normal. Parri told us you were due in. We don't need a telephone with Parri around."

"I got here."

Bobby chose a chair by the fireplace and looked at Penny on an ottoman, ready to lean back against Josh's knees when he slid in behind her. This was the way he had pictured himself and Susan as being: Susan listening to him recount his day's activities, feeding him a snack of the cake she had baked, and leaning against him with loving interest. No Keith Drayton squatting on one of their new chairs.

"But where's Susan?" Penny asked, her big brown eyes too knowing. "Why didn't you bring her over with you?"

"I told you. She was tired and went to bed."

"On the first night you're home? Now, Bobby, really!"

"Well, she did. She . . ."

"You quarreled." Penny nodded until the pink rose bobbed, then leaned forward. "You came over here for comfort, brother dear, so tell us what's wrong. Susan hasn't called off the wedding, has she?"

"I don't know." Bobby realized that he had let himself in for whatever might be coming, and it was too late to back out. Penny, like Susan, was smart; but she was family-proud, too, so he said with some courage, "We got into a hassle over Keith Drayton. He keeps right on hanging around."

"Was he there?"

"No, but he's coming tomorrow. He rigged up an excuse to drive up with Alcie, and we'll always have him on our necks." Only silence answered his hot words, so he added belligerently, "He's more than I can take."

"Well, mercy on me." To Bobby's surprise, Penny laughed. It was a soft laugh, almost a chuckle, but it put Bobby on guard. If Penny thought she could come out with any apt lines from the dozen or more plays and movies she had done she had another think coming. He was not about to be hypnotized like her audiences. "I don't intend to work hard all day," he said rigidly, "with half my mind on where Susan is or what's going on at home. I'll have to be free to work."

"Poor boy." Penny suddenly sobered as she said, "I see what you mean. You must have a free, untroubled mind in order to sell cars. And you can't, if you have to worry about Susan running around and two-timing you with Keith. That's it, isn't it?"

"Sort of."

His answer was reluctant, because he wanted to tell Penny that he had absolute trust in Susan, if not in Keith, but she was going on in the sober way that always convinced her theatre audiences. "You do have to be free, Bobby," she said. "Should you try to sell a new car to Willa Myers—and heaven knows she needs one, being divorced without much alimony—you couldn't possibly concentrate on terms while you drove around with her or bought her coffee in the drugstore, if you thought Susan had gone down to

Alcie's. And I've heard that the Tremaynes are in the market for a station wagon for the servants. Rich as they are, Kitty is apt to haggle over the price for weeks. Myra McNutt is having another one of her brooding spells, so her mother's going to buy her a car of her own. You have three good prospects right among your old girls, and they've all told me that they're holding out until you take the agency over, so I can see why you wouldn't want Susan out and running about."

"That's a little harsh, Pen," Josh said, laying his hand on her shoulder.

"I meant it to be." Penny looked at Bobby, sitting upright and uncomfortable, and said, "You may be very sure that Susan isn't going to be jealous of your old flames or keep tabs on you."

"She's already told me that."

"But neither is she going to let you lock her in a cell and pocket the key. She's got good sense, our Susan, so I wouldn't blame her if she called everything off, even at this late date."

"I wouldn't, either."

Bobby looked so miserable and contrite that Penny was tempted to cut off her lecture. Then she remembered how miserable and contrite he had always managed to look when he was small, after he had done something abominably naughty. "Butter wouldn't melt in his mouth," Trudy had said each time, when he was sorry and repentant and the family was taking a breather. All that was long in the past, however, and Bobby had seemed to grow up.

"Perhaps I should tell you something," she said thoughtfully. "It may do you some good and it may not, but I think I'll tell you. The whole family has put its collective shoulder to the wheel and has given you some tremendous wedding presents—a house, and the ground it's being built on, furniture, and a steady, reliable business."

"I appreciate it, Pen."

"But there's one thing we haven't been able to give you," she went right on. "It isn't a material thing you can touch, but it's something you can feel. And you can use it whenever you're unsure of your actions. It's the working pattern of our marriages, from Mums and Dad, straight on down."

"I know you're happy, Pen, all of you." Bobby leaned forward to offer praise and congratulations if those were what she wanted, but she was so intent on what she had decided to say that she didn't hear him.

"The basic pattern of each, Bobby, is trust. Complete and loving trust. Does that sink in?"

"Yes." Bobby looked down at his hands, studying them as if they were strangers to him, and said uncomfortably, "I get the message, Pen. I've watched all of you in action, but you've got to remember one thing. You've all worked at the business," he said, raising his head. "I'm just starting out."

"And all wrong, believe me. Let me give you an example." Penny slid out on the very edge of her ottoman, away from Josh's hand on her shoulder, then reached back for it again as she said, "When I was a kid there was a handsome young Army officer in my life who was as much older than I was as you are older than Susan."

"Yeah, I know. Terry Hayes," Bobby put in, to skip a long preliminary. "He was always hanging around. You told me all this once, but go on."

"He asked me at least a dozen times to marry him," Penny said, trying to hurry for Bobby's sake but determined to skip nothing. "But I married Josh. And Terry promptly married someone else and got a divorce, then showed up in New York. It was a matinee day, and Josh had driven out here to see about the children because they were just babies then and I hated to have them so far away. And I had an appointment to look at a furnished apartment in New York. I only had about an hour to do it, between the matinee and the evening show, so when Terry appeared backstage I was in such a hurry to get going that I took him along. We had a lot of fun, at first," she said, remembering. "Terry was as great a prankster as you are, and when the superintendent showed us the apartment and took it for granted that we were married, Terry thought it was a wonderful joke. It didn't bother me because I was concentrating on finding a home, wondering if we could fit into this one, and if the babies would wreck the beautiful furnishings. Then the super went back downstairs so I could look and think a little, and it began to get dusky and dim.

Lights came on in the city across Central Park, and before I could stop him, Terry had told me he still loved me, and had kissed me."

"Just what you think I'd do under the same circumstances, huh?"

"No." Penny could see Bobby's derisive half-smile, so she said, "The kiss isn't important, not in itself. It's the way I felt afterward, and what Josh did about it. I rushed back to the theatre all unglued. I had loved that apartment, but now I hated it. And I hated Terry for making it impossible for me to ever live there. Josh came back and found me all hunched up and crying, wretched because something ugly had come into my marriage. Oh, I know you're thinking that I didn't have to tell him," she said, seeing Bobby's quirked eyebrow, "but I did. I blurted it all out. How I felt and what Josh said to me is the only reason I'm rehashing this intimate little episode. Josh proved to me that nothing can hurt a marriage when two people are honest with each other. Somehow he made me love the apartment again and want it; and then he suggested that I write Terry a note of forgiveness, and ask him to come see our play and to have supper with us afterward. Bobby, we see Terry quite often now, every time he comes to New York, and we enjoy him a lot. But we couldn't if Josh hadn't been so wise and understanding."

"Or if Penny," Josh added modestly, "hadn't been so honest."

"Oh, pooh." Penny's rose bobbed and settled

under his chin as she leaned back against him and said, "You're always honest, too. Look at all the beautiful ladies you lunch with every whipstitch, and the hours you spend rehearsing with them—privately, in their apartments."

"I'm quite a fellow." Josh grinned at Bobby to make things easier for him, then said seriously, "Whether you're a producer, constantly thrown with young girls on their way up who don't care how homely you are if you'll only give them a boost, or whether you're an automobile salesman dealing with women who do most of the buying, your wife has to trust you. Penny and I need a double shot of trust, because I cast and direct pretty women all day and handsome leading men make love to Pen on the stage."

"Covered with make-up," Penny added, wrinkling her nose.

"We're each in business, but your Susan will be at home." Josh straightened the rose and brushed it with his lips as he said, "Don't shut her off from everyone, Bobby."

"And if you get her," Penny sat up suddenly to say, her head hitting Josh's chin so hard that his teeth snapped together, "you'd better take a good look at another marriage in our family—Peter's and Tippy's. There's no doubt but Tippy would have married Ken Prescott if he hadn't been killed, no doubt at all. She adored him, Bobby. She loved Peter, too, in a way, but there really was no one for her but Ken. Then he was killed. Peter has proved himself to be a wonderful, patient, loving guy. How would you like to have a Ken Prescott in Susan's past?"

"I couldn't take it." This was the first opportunity Bobby had had to express any opinions of his own; and while he fully understood the warning and advice that Penny and Josh had given him, he had to say honestly, "Peter came through and Tippy's crazy about him—she told me so—but I couldn't be as patient as he was. I couldn't take it if Susan still carried a secret yen for Keith."

"But Keith's living, you dope!" Penny cried. "Susan chose *you*. Can't you get that through your thick skull, and forget him?"

"I have." Bobby stood up with his hands thrust deep in his jacket pockets and told them sheepishly, "I was way ahead of you when you were halfway through your pointed tale about Terry Hayes. I was itching to go tell Susan that I've been a fool."

"Well, go do it!"

Penny bounced up, too, and began guiding him toward the door. "I don't see why you always have to be so stubborn and selfish," she scolded, not giving him time to say good night to Josh. "Now, you go right straight back to Susan's and tell her. . . . Oh, you can't, because it's so late. But be sure and do it tomorrow."

"I'll carry the ball from here on, Pen."

Bobby kissed her forehead, and Penny was sure she felt gratitude in the touch of his lips. There would have to be more lectures, warnings, and advice through the years, Bobby being as stubborn as he was, but jealousy could be ruled out. He would trust honest little Susan with his life from here on, and Penny was sure Susan would trust him.

"Oh, dear," she sighed, watching him get into his car, then going back to Josh. "I'm sure he's going to be a good boy, now—but what if Susan won't take him back?"

CHAPTER 5

BOBBY SAT IN HIS CAR outside Gladstone Gates, staring at the dark bulk of Susan's house. Once he would have driven straight into the driveway, slammed on his brakes and banged his way inside, waking anyone who wasn't in a coma. But that would have been during the years when Susan had thought him a clown and had accepted his odd performances as part of his act. Now, as both a young man in business and a partially rejected bridegroom, he was faced with a dilemma. Susan might not appreciate a midnight storming of her castle or believe that he could have such a sudden change of heart. She might not accept the simple fact that he could repent in so short a time, make a worthy decision, and stick to it for the rest of his life. Susan was very much like the girl in a musical they had seen together, he reflected glumly. The girl had sung, "Words, words, words! *Show me!*" And he didn't have three acts to do it in.

"Oh, Lord," he said now, wishing Penny had put him on the right track before he and Susan had had their hassle. He had nothing but words to offer at the moment, and showing Susan was going to take a little time—until around noon tomorrow, at least, when he could shake Keith's hand in a firm grip and say, "Glad to see you. How about coming over to our house for lunch?" That ought to show her; especially if he made Keith his best man, instead of David. Or maybe only an usher. Or maybe just made him feel especially welcome at the wedding.

Bobby sat sunk in gloom while he demoted Keith but held onto him as an important ally, and tried by wishful thinking to bring a light on in Susan's room. Nothing happened. The house remained dark and silent, so he drove lonesomely on. He would be brave, he decided, and would wait patiently until Keith came tomorrow.

But at eight o'clock the next morning, after a sleepless night, the telephone on the desk in his parents' living room drew him downstairs like a magnet. No one was up except Tippy Two, chirping like a cricket to Trudy in the kitchen, so he dialed Susan's number and sat clearing his throat while he waited for someone to answer. What should he say? He knew this approach was untimely, that he should wait until he could prove what a dear, good fellow he was, but he was too eager to hear Susan's voice. And when he did, when she answered the ringing and said, "Hello?" he became suddenly tongue-tied.

"Er—er. . . ," he mumbled, and swallowed.

To begin with his usual, "This is your bridegroom," took far too much for granted. To say, "This is Bobby, Daffy-dilly," sounded too fresh. "Lieutenant Parrish on this end," too military and like something out of a British novel. "Well," he finally did manage, "this is Robert Blaine again. Good morning."

"Oh, for heaven's sake."

Susan sounded sleepy, and since Bobby couldn't know that she had spent most of the night sitting at her window, watching his car parked at the gate, then the moon and stars, he assumed she had rested well and hated to be wakened.

"Sorry to get you up," he said, jumping the gun on his prearranged strategy, "but I—I mean the folks and I are wondering if you won't bring Alcie and Jon and Keith over to lunch today. It's a sort of family thing, you know, and they—well—they're all part of the family. I mean, Keith and his folks are—like Josh and Carrol's relatives—except that they haven't any."

"Bobby, darling, thank you." Susan understood. "You're very sweet," she said, and then she sighed. "Oh, my very dear darling," she asked, her voice quivering, "why must you always do everything the hard way? You know I don't care two little old straight pins for Keith."

"Yeah, now I do. I hadn't got the picture from both sides last night."

"But there's only one side, darling—ours. The only way we must think is together."

"How right you are," Bobby returned heartily. "It's fine by me. Good! Does that mean we still have a house and plans for next Saturday?"

"We do. Shall we go see it—our beautiful house?"

Bobby was ready to leap into space and go flying off on his little fairy wings that he was always talking about, but he remembered to stay in character and to remind soberly, "We'd have to start right away. Don't forget, we have to be back in time to bring your group over here."

And that made Susan laugh. "Bobby, you're priceless," she said. "I'm not sure if the younger ones in the group will come, because Bitsy and Vance have planned to lunch here with Anne and Keith, and Vance is furious because Anne suggested asking Davy over. He's *seething!* Bitsy's shook up and Anne's contrite. In fact, everyone is miserable but Daddy and me."

"You're happy now, aren't you, Daffy-dilly?"

"Blithely." Susan blew him a kiss that sounded like wind whistling through the receiver, then said, "I'll be ready in about half an hour. 'Bye, Bridegroom," and the connection clicked off.

"Hot diggity dog!" Bobby flung himself the length of the room and almost collided with Tippy who appeared in the hall archway.

Tippy's blonde curls were rumpled, and she regarded him through sleepy hazel eyes as she yawned and said, "I haven't slept so delightfully late in ages. Have you seen my child?"

"Trudy has her." Bobby forgot that she didn't know about his dubious marital status, so announced with a wide grin, "I'm getting married."

"Of course you're getting married. It's what we came to watch." Tippy tied the sash on her filmy white peignoir, then gently moved him out of her way as she said around another yawn, "I'll get us each a cup of coffee and we can wake up and talk while we're drinking it."

"Sorry, I've got a date."

He swung into the hall, ready to leap upstairs two steps at a time, and bumped into Peter. "Ooof," Peter said, jolted.

He wore his pajamas and robe, and looked almost as sleepy as Tippy. "What's your hurry?" he asked, running his hand through his light hair that wasn't as beautifully bright as Susan's, and blinking gray eyes that weren't half as gorgeous as her blue ones.

"Your sister." Bobby galloped on up and called over his shoulder, "We're going over to look at our house this morning, so keep everybody away. No sight-seers will be welcome."

"I get it."

Peter went on to find his own family, and Bobby did a quick job of running an electric razor over his chin. After-shave lotion was slapped on to give his skin the mannish fragrance that girls always sniffed on TV commercials, and he was ready. Susan, since she was going to live with him now, would have to grow accustomed to his old gray sweat shirt. It was all he had left from his West Point days, and if it ever wore out he intended to order another one.

"I'm bringing Alcie and Jon home to lunch," he called through his parents' closed door, and down he went.

It felt fine to drive right into Susan's driveway and pull up at the side entrance to her house. He was expected; and best of all, he was welcome. Susan wanted him, by cracky. And, oh, how he wanted Susan! It didn't matter if Keith hung around forever, because he couldn't live through another night like last night. Not another one. Not even if she treated him like an enlisted man and threw him in the guardhouse once a week. He'd march. He'd polish her old silver until his arm muscles cramped. He'd be so obedient that she'd think she had married a robot. Then the door opened and Susan came running out.

She was a dream to blind the eyes: jeans, plaid shirt, the kind that is meant to be worn with its tail hanging out, and beat-up brown loafers. The very sight of her made Bobby's heart pump so hard that he leaned out and shouted crossly, "What took you so long?"

"Breakfast." Susan climbed into the car and sat hugging her knees. "I saw you drive up," she said, "so I didn't finish. Good morning, darling."

"Good morning." Bobby's greeting came grudgingly, because he thought he might die if he didn't kiss her. "Are your folks up yet?" he asked.

"Not yet." Susan leaned over to him and put both arms around his neck. "I love you, Bobby," she whispered. Then she kissed him, far more beautifully than he knew he deserved.

Their house, when they turned onto a bumpy, rutted lane that would sometime be a winding driveway, stood on the edge of a woods. Trees hovered over it, and a small hill had been sheared off to make a turn-around beside the garage. Holes, gaping like eyes in brick walls that would be painted white, waited for casement windows to be installed, and wide matching chimneys rose from each end of the center structure. Susan had wanted a tall, stuccoed house like Gladstone Gates, but had settled for a French provincial because it would be more practical and better adapted to the many children she hoped to have. Bobby would have lived in a tent.

"It's beautiful, isn't it?" she breathed, when they were tramping up mud steps cut into what was left of the little hill, and visualizing the white retaining wall and flagstone path that would lead to their porticoed front door. "Only part of the floor is in," she warned, "so let's not go falling around and breaking our bones before Saturday."

"Wait a minute." Bobby looked at a wooden box the workmen had set before the front door and said, "You climb up and stand inside. I've got something I want to do first."

"Without me?"

"Yep, up you go."

A boost, a push, and she was standing on narrow planking, peering out and trying to see why he was skidding down the mud steps again.

"Helloooo," he called from down somewhere where she couldn't see him. "I'm home. Hey, Daffy-dilly, I'm home!" And up he came.

His arms were clasped around an imaginary bundle, and he leaned back as if whatever he carried was heavy. "You sure ordered a mess of groceries," he said, mounting the box and stretching up to kiss her. "I've been going around and around in that supermarket for over an hour. Shall I take this through to the kitchen?"

"I'll do it, darling," she said, letting him shift his burden to her. "But after we've been married a little longer," she added, "you'll find it a lot easier to drive right into the garage and come up the few steps that lead to the kitchen. I'll always be waiting for you there, instead of in our flagstoned front hall."

"Hm. Never thought of that." Bobby squeezed onto the platform beside her and looked through a long row of uprights at their left. "Good big living room," he said. "Beautiful fireplace and comfortable furniture. Nice dining room, too," he added, glancing right. "I always did like a blue dining room. And a paneled library! Wow! Shall we move on to the kitchen?"

"If we go single file." Susan balanced on a board, prepared to follow him, then gave a timid shriek. "It's the groceries," she said, when he stopped to look back. "Oh, dear, I feel so helpless. You'd better take them."

"I'll take you." Bobby scooped her up, and the shriek she gave this time was real. "You crazy dope," she shouted, while they teetered precariously above a muddy, lumber-cluttered cellar. "Put me down! If we fall through I'll *never* get to wear my wedding dress!"

"Hold still!"

Bobby began a careful walk along the plank; and abandoning all pretense of carrying groceries, Susan clutched him around the neck and tried to make herself lighter by holding her breath.

"Where in thunder is that blasted kitchen?" he asked, walking into what would be a powder room and smacking against its outer wall.

"Back out and keep on going." Susan could breathe now, because they had reached a double row of planks, and the kitchen would have a whole floor. Most of it was covered with lumber and window frames, but they couldn't fall off.

"We're here," she said thankfully, when he stood her on a neat square stack of ceramic tiles. "Oh, Bobby, dear, we lost all our groceries, but you're such a lot of fun. I'm going to love being married to you."

"Sure, Daffy-dilly? What if I stay silly most of the time?"

His anxious eyes were on a level with hers, and it didn't matter if every tile in her platform broke. "Then I'll match you," she promised. "I'll be just as silly as you are."

"Heaven help the kids." Bobby looked past the kitchen at the vague outline of a very small breakfast room, and asked thoughtfully, "Do you think we've planned on enough bedrooms?"

"Sure. Five, with two baths. Our large room and bath, and whatever's left over for them."

"That's fair enough. We can eat in the dining room and they can eat out here. There's nothing that can give you indigestion quicker than the sight of food slurping out of little mouths and splattering on the rug."

"Oh, the dogs and cats will lick everything up." Susan held out her arms and let him lift her down. "We don't have to worry," she said. "We haven't any little blessings yet, and nature has a way of giving parents nine months to prepare themselves for such a drastic change in their lives. Let's not buy a high chair until we need it."

"Suits me fine."

Bobby was eager to see the rest of the house that had now become a reality instead of a dream in blueprints, so they climbed a stairway that was made of narrow boards nailed onto a permanent structure. And it was while they were looking through another hole in an upstairs wall, straight at the white tower of Gladstone Gates shining through the trees, that he asked, "Where are we going to live until this joint's finished? And what are we going to do about a honeymoon?"

"I don't know, to both questions." Susan leaned against the wall which was rough but solid, and waited for him to go on. Bobby had had as much time to think about their future as she had, and he was a much faster thinker. Also, he knew what they could afford to do.

"I won't stay with either my folks or yours, that's for sure," he said, taking a piece of wall, too, since it was closer to her. And he mentioned casually, "There's a little apartment above the agency, about as big as a shoe box. Do you think we could squeeze in there?"

"Why not?" Susan had already seen the small apartment. She had gone with Carrol and Penny to look at it, so she said, "It's only for a couple of months, then we can rent it to somebody."

"Okay." One heavy weight had been lifted off of his mind, leaving it sagging and unbalanced under the one still left. There was the matter of the honeymoon. Brides always expected a honeymoon. He couldn't see why, because he could be just as happy with Susan in that box above the garage, saving money he didn't have, and starting in to earn some. But there it was, good old tradition.

And there was Fort Knox, too, sitting out in the Bluegrass State, waiting for him to come back and finish settling up his affairs, and to move his mess of bachelor furniture that was still cluttering up one of its BOQ's. He would have sold the furniture could he have found anyone to buy it, or would have given it away could he have found a bachelor who would take it.

"Uh—well, I'll tell you," he stammered, reluctantly, sure that Susan would give the furniture the old heave ho when she saw it, "wherever we go for a couple of weeks, we ought to double back so we'll hit Knox on our way home. I left in sort of a hurry—for just a week, you see—so I have a few more papers to sign, for travel pay and furniture shipment, and well—uh . . ."

"We honeymoon at Fort Knox." Susan had seen that coming, too. She could have told Bobby she had been prepared for it, but she only said casually, "It's fine by me. Where shall we stay? At the Guest House?"

And at that he protested so vehemently that he gave himself away. "Not on your life," he declared. "Max and Jean Osborn are going on leave and want to lend us their house. It's nice, and we can go straight out and stay there. Or in Louisville, at the Brown," he offered, prepared to do it right.

But Susan chose to accept the Osborns' less expensive hospitality. "We'll use Max and Jean's," she said, leaning against him in pleasant anticipation. "I've seen it. I went to a party there, remember?"

"Yes, but I didn't behave very well."

"You will, this time. You'll devote yourself exclusively to me, and you'll take me out to dinner, and dancing, and wherever I want to go—which will be mostly over to Tippy's. We'd better finish our tour now, if we want to make the luncheon on time."

Bobby didn't want to be anywhere but right where he was at this minute, but he walked more planks with Susan holding onto the back of his sweat shirt. And when they were out in the mud again, they both stopped to look back at the beautiful house that was theirs, and Susan said softly, "I was going to suggest that we not bother with a wedding trip."

"A honeymoon," he corrected.

"Oh, yes, a honeymoon. Excuse me." Then she smiled and said, "What has to be done, has to be done. Fort Knox, here we come again."

CHAPTER 6

"HOW ABOUT GOING OUT and sitting on the terrace until someone comes?" Bitsy had made the suggestion several times during the last half-hour, but neither Anne nor Vance had bothered to answer her.

Anne was playing the grand piano that filled a corner of the living room by the hall door, and Vance was leaning on it, admiring the way her small hands flashed up and down the keyboard. That she hit any number of wrong notes and tossed in sour chords of her own bothered them not at all. Whenever she could stay on a tune without faltering they sang together; Vance, in what his glee club teacher called a "rich baritone," and Anne taking high notes like a bird on the wing. They were so absorbed and busy nodding approval to each other that they wouldn't have heard Bitsy had she shouted.

"I asked you," Bitsy tried again, tired of listening to both vocal and instrumental discords, so going over to give Vance a punch, "if you want to go outdoors."

"Nope."

They answered together without losing a note, although Anne bobbled her bass, so Bitsy went back to the center of the room where she could watch the driveway through the open front door and Gladstone through a side window.

It didn't seem fair, she sympathized with herself, that she should have to be the one to spirit Keith off somewhere where Bobby couldn't attack him, and at the same time entertain Davy, in order to keep Vance's love life smooth. *She* hadn't invited either of them. Anne had thrust Davy upon them, being selfish and self-centered, and Keith had simply announced that he was coming. Naturally, he had put a question mark on the end of his announcement, but he had a right to be here. He was helpful and pleasant, and he didn't stand about like Davy, looking smug and as if he ought to be smoking a pipe.

Davy, she told herself disgustedly, would probably do exactly that in a year or two. He would copy the way his father often stood, leaning against a mantel and pointing his pipe at people while he told them what they should or should not do for the good of the family. Then she was ashamed. David Parrish was so trustworthy and good. He was always ready to pitch in and help, not to just point, so perhaps his son had better sense than he seemed to have. At least he hadn't wanted to come today, and he wouldn't if his mother hadn't said he must. It was all a sorry mess, and it had been dumped right into Elizabeth Jordon's lap.

"Well, those are all the songs I know without my music," Anne said, stopping the infernal din and giving Bitsy a chance to walk over and pluck her off the piano bench. But Vance hustled to plop himself down beside her and start a crashing duet of chopsticks.

Away they went again, laughing and looking at each other. Anne was enjoying Vance—until Davy came. And glaring at her, Bitsy lost her admiration for Anne that had amounted almost to adoration. Anne had been her first friend at Briarcliff, the first to risk coming home with a girl whom the other students considered dull and snippily British. The first to say "Bitsy" instead of the stiff, dignified "Elizabeth" that Bitsy disliked, the first to teach her to dance. Anne had been Bitsy's sponsor. But watching her being so silly now, Bitsy decided that she had more than repaid Anne by giving her delightful weekends at Gladstone Gates.

"I'm going outside," she shouted, desperate enough to go out and torture the garden, breaking off chrysanthemums or pulling up the plants by their roots if they were too contrary to give up their blossoms. "You can just hide in here and let everybody be angry." And out she marched.

Fortunately for the chrysanthemums, she couldn't see in two directions if she sat down in the path, and she didn't want to risk a run in her new nylons by kneeling. So she stood staring at the sunlit countryside. What if Susan and Bobby should come tearing in before she could lure Keith off somewhere to hide him, she worried, remembering the way Susan had raced upstairs last night, and still hearing the sobs that had drifted out of Susan's open window and into hers. She might never wear her golden maid-of-honor dress. And what if she couldn't sidetrack Davy? The Fourth of July fireworks in the village square would be a mild display compared to the countdown and explosions at the Jordons'.

The bright September sun beat down on her while she stood watching and waiting, turning her into a bright pink flower caught in a sea of yellow. Then to her sudden horror, she saw Keith's car follow Bobby's through the gate. And as if that weren't enough, Davy appeared between the trees, making his reluctant way across the grass.

"Oh, mercy on us," she groaned, and sank down out of sight.

Bobby and Susan hopped out, looking awful. Susan made a ghastly bride in jeans, and Bobby had a three-cornered tear in his pants. Bitsy took a peek and waited to see what they would do. Keith was alone. No Alice and Jonathan were with him, and Bitsy wanted to cover her ears and miss the explosion.

But none came. Bobby surprised her by walking back and calling pleasantly as he went, "Hi there. We've been over looking at our new house," he went on, much too low for Bitsy to hear, "and were afraid you'd get here before we did. Where're Alcie and Jon?"

"Coming along in their car." Keith stepped out and gripped Bobby's extended hand firmly as he explained, "I have to go back to Princeton, so we came in a two-car convoy. Congratulations."

"Thanks."

Bobby managed to hook his other arm possessively through Susan's, but Keith freed his hand and took her by both shoulders. "You look radiant," Bitsy strained to hear him say. "I'm glad for you, Susan."

He sounded sincere, and Susan's smile was relaxed as she leaned confidently against Bobby. "I suppose everything is under control," Bitsy told the happy little faces of the spared chrysanthemums, her nervous shaking temporarily slowing to march time. "Susan must have spoken quite a piece this morning." And then she watched Alcie and Jon drive in, just as Davy crossed the driveway.

Bitsy knew she was a coward. Unexpected squabbling could start a flutter inside her chest which gradually spread to her hands and feet, paralyzing them and making them completely useless. And because she always looked so statue-calm, the silly knocking of her heart against her ribs annoyed her far more than it did those who often stared at her and thought her cold.

How to rescue Keith, who wanted to be rescued? What to do with Davy, who didn't know he presented a problem? Bitsy cowered among the flowers, conscious that the piano had stopped, and so vainly hoping that Vance would come out if only to behave insultingly. Then the ones in the driveway all bent over to look at something Alcie held in her cupped hands, and she scrambled up and streaked for the house.

"What became of him?" she demanded, when the screen door had slammed shut behind her and she saw Anne sitting alone on the piano bench, turned to watch what was going on outside.

"I don't know." Anne shrugged and slid around to say, "He took one look at Davy and muttered something about nobody telling him that that white-sidewalled kid was coming, and dashed out through the hall. I think he went upstairs, but I couldn't see. Something thumped up there, like a bed falling down."

"Oh, dear," Bitsy knew she would have to go up. She couldn't wait for Susan to quietly make Vance behave like a host. Keith and Davy would be coming in, perhaps the others with them, and then it would be too late to talk to Susan. "Vance did so know," she declared. "He was right here when Susan telephoned Davy's mother."

"No, he wasn't. He really wasn't." Anne shook

her head and said miserably, "I wish I'd never seen Davy Parrish!"

"And don't you think *I* wish you hadn't?" The curving stairway was waiting for Bitsy's feet to mount it, but she still stood, saying, "It's all very easy for you. You can stay down here blinking your eyes at Davy. I'm the one Vance is quite apt to knock about," she added, trying to work up a good case of anger that would last her through her coming siege with Vance.

"Oh, Bitsy, I'm so sorry." Anne truly was, but there was nothing she could do. The screen door was already opening and Bitsy had fled through the hall.

No blood found its way down to Bitsy's wobbly legs. Her heart hadn't the strength to pump out any, she thought, peeking timidly through Vance's partly open door. He was sitting on the end of the bed that still had enough slats left in to hold it up, and was busily cleaning a gun.

"Oh, Vancey, *don't,*" she squeaked, so frightened that she fell into the room and threw herself down in front of him. "You mustn't think of doing that!"

"Doing what?" He looked up with an oily rag in mid-air, and she tried to snatch the gun away from him.

"Oh, don't kill Davy," she begged, "or Anne, or anybody. You can't go to jail when we have a wedding coming up. Please, please, don't go balmy *now!*"

Had Vance felt like laughing, he would have

whooped right then. Trust Bitsy to pop off with a British word like "balmy." "This is an air rifle, silly," he said, seeing that she was really in a state. "Old man Potter's dogs have been coming over here and picking on Cassius, so I promised Ellin to give them a burst of BB shot. My gosh, stop crying."

"I—c-can't." Bitsy was prostrate with her face hidden in the bright red bedspread. "I—I was so—so—frightened," she wept. "You get so mad, and I thought . . ."

"Aw, come on." Vance was about to lift her up, but her words reminded him that if he coaxed her back downstairs he would have to go with her. "You'd better go on," he said. "I'm not wanted."

"But I want you, Vancey." Bitsy looked up, her cheeks tear-stained. "Anne wants you, too," she added loyally, since she was certain that her own need wouldn't affect him. "She's sorry Susan invited Davy. She is, Vance, truly. She's sunk."

"Oh, yeah?" Vance had made up his mind to go out and take pot shots at stray dogs, and to eat his lunch in the kitchen. He wasn't going to join the merry little group downstairs, not even if Bitsy flattened herself before him and beat a tattoo on the floor with her head. Let Anne beam on Davy until he melted down like a wax candle in the sun. Vance Jordon had walked out, and he didn't intend to walk back in. He couldn't. Not with a little sister tugging him along by the hand and piping proudly, "Here he is, I've got him."

"You go on," he said, reaching down among the bed slats for a clean rag and finally yanking it out from under her. "I've got my day planned."

"Oh, Vancey." Bitsy's tears began to flow again because, suddenly, she loved him so much. He was such a dear, mistreated brother. He was all she would have left after next Saturday, and she wanted him to be happy. She wanted the two of them to be as close as Susan and Neal were. To be twins, to be . . . "Oh, horrors!" she cried.

"Now, what?" Vance wanted to give her a push so he could go on cleaning his gun, but he waited.

"Neal!" Bitsy said, looking up. "You were supposed to be at West Point in time to pick up Neal right after chapel. It's after twelve o'clock and you haven't even started! Oh, Susan will die. She'll go to Aunt Marjorie's and she won't see Neal. . . ."

"I'll go right away." Vance was glad to toss his gun on the bed and spring up. "Thanks for reminding me," he said. "I'll sneak out and take Alcie's car, and if anybody asks where I've gone, don't tell 'em."

"But you will come back?" Bitsy interrupted the alterations he was hastily making in his plans to ask, "You'll deliver Neal, then come back here?"

"I may." He had a legitimate reason, even an imperative one, to come down from the second floor, so he left her sitting with the barrel of a broken gun in her back, and said as he hustled out, "I'll probably be late, so go on and eat without me. The Parrishes will feed me, so go on and eat."

He was on his way down, and she was still up. He was off to tell his grievances to Neal, and here she sat, tear-stained and rumpled, and with a long smear of grease on her skirt. It wasn't fair. It wasn't.

"Oh, well, chin up, old girl," she finally mumbled, getting stiffly to her feet. "You really wanted Vance to stay away, you know you did."

It took her several minutes more to change into another dress, to wash her face and apply fresh lipstick; and by the time she got downstairs again only Anne and Keith and Davy were left in the living room. Anne looked inquiringly at her, but she only said, "Hello, Keith. Hello, Davy," and let Anne worry. Why make everything so simple for Anne by explaining that Vance had gone off on a forgotten errand?

The luncheon, when finally ready, was unlike anything Davy would have at Gladstone or the beautiful parties Jenifer gave in England. Ellin was at her wits' end with Donna who didn't know a cream pitcher from a tin cup, who argued that paper napkins would do just as well for kids as linen ones, who piled silverware and plates on the biggest tray she could find, around bread, salad, cold turkey and ham, expecting guests to hunt through the heap for what they wanted.

The beautiful embroidered place mats from the Philippines were crooked on the dining-room table, empty boxes that had held wedding gifts were still stacked on the seats of the chairs; and by the time Bitsy could slip out to the kitchen Ellin had firmly closed her bedroom door and refused to come out again until Donna had been removed from her sight forever.

So a picnic was set up on the terrace. Donna clip-clopped up the back stairway with a floor mop and the laundry she had forgotten to put away yesterday, Ellin was placated, and everyone pitched in to carry the lunch outside. The sunshine was warm, the air flower-scented, and Plush and Cassius arrived in a hurry. There was no jellied consommé with thin slices of lemon and Ellin's famous cornsticks to start off with. Instead, sandwiches were made as they were needed, an inch thick and with the crusts left on. Milk was poured from the dairy bottle it came in, and iced tea from a pitcher with a chipped lip. Plush and Cassius had a heyday. They ate everything that was fed to them, or dropped or spilled, then licked the plates of melting ice cream and cake.

"They make me think of the woman who hired a new cook," Keith said, picking up the shining clean plate Cassius had left when he moved on to Davy. "The girl was a mess. Just about like Donna," he said, lowering his voice, "and after a week the woman couldn't take it any longer, so went out to the kitchen to fire her. She had paid her off and was starting out when she saw the cook lay two dollars of her salary on the table.

'What's that for?' the woman asked. And the cook answered, 'Why, it's for the dog. He washed all the dishes.'"

"Ugh." Bitsy laughed with the others but she quickly picked up her plate while it still had a smear of ice cream on it. It would be just like Donna to decide it was clean and put it away.

Davy talked very little but he was a good listener. His blue eyes studied Anne when she was hopping about being helpful, and he had a shy, sweet smile whenever anyone spoke directly to him. He didn't look like a solemn pipe smoker today, and Bitsy wondered why she had never really noticed him before. She had played tennis at Gladstone, always with David, doing her level best to beat him, and sometimes succeeding. She had swum in the Gladstone pool, but never with Davy lounging about, although the pool had been built after he had come home from Warm Springs and was part of his physical therapy. Davy always came to family gatherings but stayed off in a corner talking to Vance. Vance had said he was "a really swell guy," and, until yesterday, had liked being with him. It made her sad to think that through no fault of his own Davy had lost a friend.

"Hm?" she said, suddenly realizing that Keith had asked her a question.

"Woof woof," Keith barked. "That means, 'want me to go out and wash the dishes?' I'm not exactly hungry now, but I'll give it a try."

"Let's go look at Susan's house instead," she

suggested. "No one will be there, and it's a beautiful day to go climbing about."

"But I have to go back to school." Anne looked doubtfully at Bitsy as she added, "Vance said he'd drive me over so perhaps I'd better wait for him."

"You might wait all night." Bitsy knew that Vance would come home only when he got good and ready, and, personally, she hoped it wouldn't be soon. It would do Anne good to think she had lost him. "Keith will drop you off on his way back to Princeton," she said, without stopping to think. And then she wanted to snatch the words back. This might very well be the last she would ever see of Keith. His heart was mending so nicely from Susan that it was risky to let Anne sew a few experimental stitches on it. "I mean, if you can stay until tonight," she added in a rush. "Keith won't be going back until tonight, I hope."

"Not if Susan and Bobby invite me to stay," Keith answered innocently. "I really came up to give them their choice of two wedding presents I found, but I haven't had a chance to, yet."

He grinned openly at each of them, but Bitsy thought she could read disappointment in his eyes. Why, this party is just kid stuff to him, she suddenly realized. If Vance had been here it wouldn't have seemed so frightfully young to him, or if Neal had been around, or even Daddy. How could I have expected him to spend a whole day with a bunch of high school teen-agers?

Her gay fine plans had flopped, just as they so often did, because of her own stupidity and willfulness, and she stood up purposefully. "I'll take you over to Aunt Marjorie and Uncle Dave's, Keith," she said, not caring what it might do to Bobby's afternoon. "You've been awfully nice to stay with us so long."

"But, Bitsy, child, it's what I wanted to do. I was invited to the Parrishes." Keith put the plate he was holding on the tray and got up to stand above her. "Look, doll," he said, using the pet name he had given her the winter before, "I'm in no hurry to pass along a lamp or a set of *demitasse* cups. I've got plenty of time and I'd like to take a look at Susan's house."

"With us, not—not with Susan?" Bitsy asked, looking up at him.

"Why not? A house is a house, whoever shows it to you, and a gorgeous Sunday afternoon is made to be enjoyed. Let's go look at the house."

"Well . . ." Bitsy could see Anne grinning at her like a little demon, and there was something so pleased and satisfied in Anne's expression that she loved her again. "And we might drive by and pick Vance up," she said, wanting to be kind to Anne, too. "And after we've all seen the house we can come back here."

"Count me out," Davy said quickly, having known ever since he came that he had spoiled a planned foursome and wondering how he could leave. "I'm no good at climbing, you know," he explained, hating every word he spoke, because he was admitting to others something that he vehemently denied to himself. "Just drop me off when you pick up Vance."

"Are you sure, Davy?" Bitsy looked across at him, a little sorry to be rid of him so conveniently, but more thankful than sorry. Keith came first. Keith needed someone older along, and Anne had to get Vance back. "Are you sure you don't mind?" she asked, too eagerly.

"I promised Lang I'd go to the movies with him." Davy stood up, too, resting his weight on his good leg while he shook the crumbs in his napkin down to the seemingly hollow Cassius.

He wanted to leave, and quickly. Plans were being made to exclude him, and he understood why. He didn't belong with girls. For a few minutes during lunch he had thought he did because Anne had said that she would love to come to Gladstone and ride with him. "You won't make fun of me, will you?" Anne had asked, twinkling her dimples. "I'm a terrible rider, you know, and everyone has told me how wonderful you are."

No, he didn't belong, so why try to promote a friendship with Anne? He couldn't dance, and she was the dancing, butterfly type. "I'll walk on home," he said. "Lang didn't go to Grandpa's so he'll be waiting for me. Good-bye, Ann. Good-bye, Keith. Thanks, Bitsy, for a swell time."

"But Davy!" Bitsy was on her feet, too, and she felt ashamed and sick inside. She felt as she had long, long ago when a younger child had come to play and she had sent her home because she interfered with a game that was too old for her. Jenifer had been stern with her, that time, but there was no Jenifer here to make her run after Davy and coax him back. So she only followed him to the steps and said politely, "I'm awfully sorry you have to go. I'll see you tomorrow night at Penny's."

"Sure thing."

Davy did his best not to limp as he skirted the rose hedge, and he forced himself to turn back and wave. "Is this the way it's always going to be?" he asked the trees and sky before him, unable to believe that age had been his handicap, not his infirmity. And his heart cried out to be like other boys, like Lang who could hang by his heels on a trapeze. Davy didn't know that the courage it took to walk away was a far greater accomplishment than hanging by his heels.

"I feel awful," Bitsy said, still not calling to Davy to come back. "We did invite him over."

"But he said he had to go home." Anne wanted to make her peace with Vance. Davy had seemed attractive yesterday, with his millionaire parents in the background, but he really was too young. She knew it now; and because she hadn't so much as noticed his limp, she said, "Stop worrying, Bits. I'll hunt up one of the younger girls at school and ask him over. I'll bet he'd like Mary Beth Hughes."

"Perhaps." Bitsy hated her selfishness that kept cropping up. "Yes, I rather suppose he would," she said, wishing Keith would say something that would ease her conscience. But he was piling more soiled plates on the tray. "Don't bother with all that," she said irritably. "I'll send Donna out." And she ran inside to find Ellin and to tell her what had happened.

"I did it again," she said, letting the dining-room door swing shut behind her and standing straight and tall against it. "I was selfish and horrid again, just as I was last winter. I let Davy go home with his feelings hurt. I haven't improved at all, have I?"

"Ah, child, for shame." Ellin looked up from the newspaper she had been reading at the table, and said gently, "'Tis said that if ye know ye're wrong 'tis some improvement. And if ye admit it, 'tis even more. Are ye sure ye hirt the lad?"

"Oh, I'm sure." Bitsy walked over to the table, welcoming the scolding and ready to provide evidence against herself. "I've been mad off and on all day," she said, "but I liked Davy, and I wanted him to come—and then I got tired of him and wanted him to go home. I wanted him out of the way, I suppose, just as I wanted Susan out of the way last winter so I could take over her job in the bookshop. I knew it, but I didn't care."

"Dear, dear, whin ye wire doin' so will," Ellin said, sighing and shaking her head; and then she suggested, "but sometimes a thing can be mended, if ye try hard enough."

"Uhhuh, that's exactly what I was telling myself," Bitsy put in, "when I let Davy go home.

Only I was referring to mending Keith's broken heart. I thought—and I still think, Ellin—that Keith is more important than Davy. He is, you know."

"To you and himsilf, pirhaps. To the rist of the world? I doubt it."

"So I've spoiled things again," Bitsy condemned herself miserably. "I'm sure you won't want to call me 'lovey' now. I've lost the right to be called that," she said around a sigh, remembering how hard she had worked to be worthy of the coveted endearment. "Just Susan will be 'lovey' again."

"Why should she be?" Ellin asked tartly. "Ye earned the title once, so why should a little backslidin' rob ye of it? I'm not of a changeable mind."

"Thank you, but I don't deserve it." Bitsy sighed again, then gently smoothed the top of Ellin's gray hair. "Please don't ever stop calling me lovey," she begged in a whisper. "I'll keep trying ever so much harder."

"I know ye will." Ellin reached up a workworn hand to pull Bitsy around where she could smile at her and say, "Ye must hurry back to ye're other guists now. We'll have plinty of time to talk." And she added slyly but sweetly, "Run on now, lovey."

CHAPTER 7

BITSY STARTED DOWN THE STAIRWAY with her school books and saw Susan sitting on the bottom step. Susan had the telephone in her lap and the New York classified directory open beside her.

"Oh, good morning, Bits," she said, looking up and leaving the number half-dialed. "I'm trying to find someone to take Donna's place."

"Is she gone?"

"Vance took her home half an hour ago. None of the agencies are open yet, and I've got to find somebody today." Susan moved over for Bitsy to pass, and said with a discouraged headshake, "I know I won't have time to help Ellin, and with the whole bunch coming here to dinner Wednesday night, and with Alcie and Jon coming back and staying until Sunday . . ."

"Let Alcie help," Bitsy broke in to suggest. "I'll do what I can after school, but why can't Alcie take over? She's a Jordon; and from what you've told me, you all pitched in for her wedding."

"But haven't you heard?" Susan slammed the directory shut and said, looking pleased, "She's going to be a mother. She and Jon are walking on air, and her doctor said that, if she'll just stay quiet, she'll get the baby."

"I didn't even get to see Alcie." Bitsy walked on toward the dining room and her breakfast, saying loftily, "If you'll remember, none of you ever came home, and Keith finally had to leave with your wedding present still in the back of his car."

"Oh, golly, wasn't that thoughtless?"

Susan hopped up to put the telephone back, and as she followed Bitsy to the table and took the chair opposite her, she said, "You had quite a day, didn't you?"

"What makes you say that?"

She took a careful swallow of her orange juice, alert and ready to defend poor, forgotten Keith, but Susan only said, "I heard you and Vance hassling in his room when I ran upstairs to change my clothes to go to the Parrishes'. I'd have gone on back to straighten him out but I was in a hurry. And Ellin told me you sent Davy home."

"I didn't exactly send him," Bitsy defended, surprised by the curve the conversation had rounded. "He went. I suppose I could have kept him," she said, sprinkling sugar on her cereal and not looking up. "Then Vance could have stayed mad, and Keith could have stayed bored, and I could have done exactly what you did—not given a whoop."

"Oh, Bits, you don't believe that." Susan looked across the table. "It was a family day," she explained, "with everyone invited to Penny's for dinner. It was my first bridal party. Bobby's parents and Daddy were having such a wonderful time—everyone was—and even Davy and Lang showed up. Everybody was there but you."

"And I suppose you hold that against me."

"No." Susan moved the salt and pepper shakers about as if they were pawns in a chess game while she said slowly, "I do appreciate your being nice to Keith. He can come to other parties if he wants to but he wouldn't have been happy at this one. Daddy gave Bobby and me the deed to our land, and the others all had the receipted bills for our house and furniture wrapped up in silly packages. It was wonderful."

"I'm glad somebody had fun."

Bitsy managed to sound abused, even though she was still dreamy from the last three hours of her day. Vance had finally come home to take Anne back to school, and she and Keith had eaten a cozy dinner before the fire, on TV tables. No one had been there to interrupt their steady exchange of confidences. Bitsy was convinced that she had been completely adult and unbiased while she criticized Susan's careless behavior of the morning. And, after sympathy and coaxing, she had broken down and told how difficult both Susan and Vance had made it for her.

Softly glowing embers had helped her halting tale along, and Keith's dark eyes had sparked encouragement. He thought her noble and brave to have sent Davy on his way, and had frankly said so. He might even have added a light, complimentary kiss, if Ellin hadn't come in to bring more cake.

"I have to go to school, now," she said to Susan, still dreamily believing that nothing is so good for one's morale as an hour's exposure to another's honest admiration. It's like a sun bath. And while it may be followed by an even longer period of burning doubt, as hers had been, Bitsy was sure it was worth it. "I'm sorry if I hurt Davy's feelings," she said, "but it wasn't entirely my fault. I'm not going to work in Ye Book Nook this week, so I'll come straight home from school to help you."

"Oh, I'll have someone by afternoon," Susan answered confidently, wondering what was going on in Bitsy's mind.

If she lived to be a hundred, she would never understand Bitsy. It's queer, she mused listening to Bitsy take her blue denim school jacket from the hall closet, how children in the same family can be so different. It's almost as if all the traits to be inherited are shaken up in a grab bag, and each child reaches in and draws out a handful. Some of the Jordons had drawn many of the same traits and so could understand each other, as she and Neal and Alcie did, while others . . . She broke off as Bitsy came back again.

"Why don't you get on the phone and hunt up Rosie?" Bitsy suggested. "She's been wanting to come back to us ever since you left Governors Island, and Ellin's quite accustomed to fussing at her. She could catch a train from Washington and be here in a few hours."

"Rosie? Oh, mercy!" Susan could remember Rosie better than Bitsy could. Rosie was a happy mess. She had bright pink cheeks and black fly-away hair that looked electrically wired. Her clothes were never quite coupled together and her stockings were always wrinkled.

"She was faithful to Gwenn when Gwenn was sick," Bitsy reminded, while Susan still hesitated. "She stayed down in Pennsylvania with Gwenn and put up with her tantrums for six whole months. And she hates living in a furnished room and doing day work."

"But will she want to go home again?" Susan asked doubtfully. "What will you do with her after I leave?"

"Ship her back." Bitsy was far less tender-hearted than Susan, and besides, she was in a hurry. "She'll get to see your wedding," she said, "and she'll think she's in Heaven. If you've got any sense you'll call her."

Bitsy had no more time to waste, so she left

Susan nodding like a mandarin and hurried down the hill to the crossroads where the bus to Briarcliff stopped. Vance rarely took the bus now that the family had two cars, and he rarely invited Bitsy to ride with him. So she climbed aboard with other students and housewives on their way to market, and found herself wishing that Davy would be on this bus, instead of on the one which passed behind the stables of Gladstone.

She had decided to apologize to Davy, to tell him frankly that she knew how rude she had been and how deeply she regretted it. The whole business was a nuisance but both her conscience and Keith had told her it must be done. It was unfortunate that she couldn't blurt it all out on a bus, instead of having to waste a whole hour after school.

"I feel sorry for Davy," she screamed at Anne at lunchtime, above the babble of three hundred voices in the dining room. "And I'm ripping mad at you for the way you made me treat him."

"*Me?*" Anne screamed back, astounded.

"Yes, you. Nothing would do but that Susan should call up and ask Davy over, and it ruined the whole day. *I'm* the one who got into trouble."

"Well, I never heard of anything so silly!" Anne's voice was incredulous. She had Vance back, and Bitsy had had a whole long evening alone with Keith, so she couldn't see what all the fuss was about. "Vance says . . ." she began; but Bitsy had pushed back a stemmed glass of rice pudding and was standing up.

"Vance, Vance, Vance," she said, leaning across the table so she wouldn't have to shout. "I'm fed up with Vance and you can tell him so if you like." And with a toss of her head, she marched out.

She knew Anne was staring speechlessly after her but she didn't care. Anne must be punished, too. Since she lacked a conscience, let her live with worry. Let her wonder if the extra twin bed at Bitsy's would be hers for the weekend, if she would sit with the bride's family on Saturday afternoon or have to come to the wedding in the Briarcliff station wagon, crowded in with the headmistress and six of Susan's favorite teachers.

"Bitsy, wait!" she heard Anne call, but she didn't stop.

She hurried from one class to another all afternoon, not really as angry with Anne as with herself for having been led like a stupid sheep into this pen of disaster; and when school was over, she climbed aboard the bus that went near Davy's instead of on her own, looking hopefully along the aisle. But Davy wasn't there. Most of the seats were vacant, so she chose one and sat down, her books on her lap.

Bitsy was adept at spinning daydreams. She could spend hours, or only minutes, if that was all the time she had, making a successful occasion of something she was going to do. People behaved exactly as she wanted them to, then, and she always ended up the heroine. Susan's wedding, for instance. The setting for her dream was always on the side lawn beyond the garden, where the green grass and trees blended into Gladstone's parkland. And Keith was always waiting for her there. He always sat on a stone bench far away from everyone, looking lonely and disconsolate, and waiting patiently for her, no matter how long she took to charm her father's guests. She could see him as she moved about from group to group. Some groups told her what a darling she was to look after them so beautifully, others said how lucky her father was to have such a lovely little hostess still at home. People detained her to praise, compliment and admire her; and it always took quite a while to make sure that the caterer's staff was functioning properly, that Gwenn was behaving, and Alcie was resting under one of the woven reed umbrellas David had sent over. But at last she would be free to go out to Keith.

The dream usually varied from there on, but it always had the same ending. Sometimes Keith was morose and threatening to turn vagabond, sometimes he was merely despondent and clinging to her hand. But whether he paced or slumped, he never failed to come out of their little session triumphant and eager to become the world's foremost scientist, and vowing that he owed it all to her.

The dream today was different. Davy had to be the second character in it, and she couldn't set her scene because she had no idea where she might find him. Vance had often said that he rode his horse after school, but what if he had caught an earlier bus, already saddled up and gone? Or what if he should be just leaving? Talking to him face to face on the ground would be much easier and safer, she thought, than looking up at him astride his horse. How could she think what she wanted to say while she dodged four prancing feet and a swinging rear end?

Bitsy was afraid of horses. And when the bus let her off at the entrance to a long lane, she stepped down reluctantly and stood looking at the red-tiled roofs of the Gladstone stables in the distance. Perhaps Davy hadn't come home yet, and she could sit down under a wild cherry tree and wait. Then she remembered that the Academy always closed earlier than Briarcliff, and started walking.

Davy, with his horse, was just coming into a bricked courtyard when she reached it, but he was leading the big animal, not riding it. Everything smelled too rural to suit Bitsy's delicate nostrils, although the cow barns were far in the distance and the work horses were grazing in a large pasture. Anything that she might have planned to say would be wasted, because the whole scene was unfamiliar and Davy didn't look like Davy.

He wore a tweed riding coat over a white shirt that was open at the throat, light whipcord breeches and tan riding boots; and with a beagle puppy snuffling along behind his bay hunter he looked like a young country squire.

"Well, hi," he said, surprised to see her in such an out-of-the-way place. And he asked curiously, "How come you're back here?"

"I wanted to apologize for yesterday," Bitsy said loudly, not wanting to go too close. "You were put in a frightful spot and I didn't know what to do about it."

"Forget it." Davy walked over to her, the big brown horse following docilely along at the end of the reins; and seeing her step back, he said, "Singing Star's a gentle guy. You wouldn't hurt her, would you, Sing?" he asked, hooking an arm over the horse's neck and holding a piece of sugar out to Bitsy. "Give him this and he'll love you forever."

Bitsy reached out hesitantly to take the sugar between her thumb and forefinger, but Davy flattened her palm and placed the lump on it. "Now give it to him," he said.

It made something squirm along Bitsy's spine to feel soft, velvety lips nibbling at her hand, but she bore it. The incident of yesterday seemed to have been pushed completely out of the picture and she would have to bring it back. "I'm really sorry, Davy," she said, when Sing had stopped sniffing her hand and was nuzzling at Davy's pocket. "I've hated myself ever since."

"You shouldn't have."

"And Ellin scolded me," she went on, eager to purge herself. "And Susan would have if I hadn't stopped her. Goodness knows what Daddy will say when I tell him."

She was a suppliant, and a very honest and contrite one, he thought, asking him for forgiveness when he didn't know what to say. She had walked a long way to do it, and here he stood, tongue-tied. "Gosh," he finally managed, "I didn't mind."

"Oh, but you did, Davy." Bitsy had been feeling her way along, but now she said with more confidence, "I could tell by the way you walked off. I walk that way myself when I'm embarrassed. Quite stiff and with my back straight."

David wanted to tell her he always walked that way when he was trying not to limp, but the words wouldn't come out. His bitterness over the limp was his secret. "It's really okay," he said. And because she wouldn't believe he was speaking the truth, that yesterday had been no worse than all the other days when he couldn't swim in a nearby lake with the gang, or go hiking in shorts, or join the Boy Scouts, he said, "Why don't you come up to the house? I don't have to ride today. Lang's going out, and he can lead Sing for exercise."

"Are you sure you wouldn't rather ride?"

Bitsy almost preferred staying with Davy to going home and helping Susan. She hadn't had a chance to explain to him that while his age was against him now, it was something he would outgrow in time, and that there were a number of nice, younger girls about, so he mustn't be discouraged. Somebody has to tell him the facts of life, she thought, waiting while he led Singing

Star back into the stable and talked briefly to someone, probably Lang.

"All set," he said, coming out and taking her books.

The sunlight shone on his wavy blond hair, and walking along beside him Bitsy was surprised to see how much taller he was than she. He didn't look at all like a little boy to whom she could talk in a kind, motherly way.

They followed another graveled lane that would lead them past a garage larger than Bitsy's whole house. A few apple trees left from an old orchard grew along the way, and Davy asked, "Want an apple?"

"I'd love one," she said; and then she looked at the trees. They grew on the other side of a deep ditch and beyond a split-rail fence. If Davy couldn't walk about in a half-finished house, she suddenly realized, he could never manage that ditch; and she said impulsively, "I'll get them."

"Why?" He gave her a long, cool stare that she couldn't answer. Then, even while she stabbed helplessly at elusive words, he had laid her books on the grass and was in the ditch and up again, and over the fence. He did it as quickly as Vance or Lang could, and it made her wonder why there was always such a fuss made about "poor Davy's affliction."

"Take your choice," he said, coming back and holding out four bright red balls. "Dad's been feeding the trees so these ought to be good."

"Let's sit here and eat them." Bitsy's books were

on the bank by the ditch, and she sat down beside them. She would be in the midst of uninterrupted quiet here with David anchored beside her. Circumstances would force him to listen to a lecture on his youth, if only she could think of some way to begin. He was taking large bites from his apple, and it seemed as if he could be silent as long as she could. "What makes you so shy?" she asked suddenly.

"I'm not shy," he answered, tossing the core across the road.

"Then stuffy, or whatever you are."

"I'm not that, either." He grinned at her and offered her another apple, but since she hadn't finished the one she had, he rubbed it along his own jacket sleeve and said, "At least I don't mean to be."

"Well, you are. Sometimes you look at people as if you find them frightfully boring and would like to bash some sense into them." That was the last thing Bitsy had expected to say. She had planned to reassure and bolster poor, pitiful little Davy, not to scold him. But poor, pitiful little Davy had disappeared, and this boy sitting beside her was nine months older than she and a stranger to her. "I'm not *stupid*," she flared.

"Who said you were?" He laughed then, and twirled the apple around by its brown sprig of stem, watching it revolve as he said thoughtfully, "It's queer that we can never quite put ourselves across to other people, isn't it? *We* know who and what we are, but we never seem able to make the other fellow see it. At least, I can't. Mom says I'm antisocial because of my polio, and Dad says it's all part of the teens. He says he was completely antisocial when he was sixteen."

"I don't believe it."

"Well, he says so. And Mom agrees that he wasn't so hot when she first knew him. But whatever he was," David said quietly, "doesn't necessarily apply to me. I'm whatever I am, and I'm sorry if I irritated you."

"Oh, you didn't, Davy." Bitsy turned and looked at him then. "I came over to tell you that you're simply too young for our group," she said, "but now I'm not so sure I was right. You seem so different and so much older today. I don't know why, but you seem so much older."

Davy was silent for a few moments, staring down at the twirling apple, then he said carefully, "You seem different, too. I appreciate your coming all this way to apologize for something that didn't need any apology, so perhaps . . ." he let the apple drop and drew his knees up to clasp his arms around them before he went on ". . . perhaps I ought to say that a lot of yesterday was my fault. I'm older than either you or Anne, so I shouldn't have been such a baby. Oh, I knew that I'd accidentally cut Vance out and made him mad, but I shouldn't have moped about it. He gave me heck last night when he showed up at Penny's, and told me I was dumb to get my feelings hurt and pull out. It's something I can't help, Bitsy, and I often wonder if I'll ever be able to."

"Why not, Davy?"

"Oh, it all goes back to my polio," he said simply. "Everybody says I was a normal kid before that happened, and for three or four years afterward. I guess I was. The whole family hovered over me, and Lang's the one who should have come out of it tied up in knots. Nobody paid any attention to him until he was a great big kid and could walk and talk, and then not much. He had two good legs, you see."

"But so have you now, Davy," Bitsy reminded, thinking of the way he had taken the ditch and swung over the fence.

"Sure."

Davy was silent while he stretched out his legs in their polished boots and studied them, and Bitsy asked, "You're healthy now, aren't you?"

"As healthy as I'm ever going to be." He had wanted for a long time to tell someone about his right leg, to talk with someone his own age who could understand what just looking at the ugly thing did to him. But perhaps Bitsy wasn't the one. She had never bothered with him until today. She wasn't really the good companion sitting here beside him in the hazy sunshine. They weren't boy meets girl on a September afternoon. She was still Bitsy Jordon who liked to show off her tennis and who had pranced back here to make a fine apology and impress her elders. Or was she? "Why did you really hunt me up?" he asked.

"Because I was sorry for what I'd done," she answered truthfully. "I do get sorry sometimes. Most of the time I'm quite selfish and horrid, but Ellin is helping me to be better. You see," she explained, "I was frightfully spoiled, too, when I was little, in England."

"Oh." If she thought him too young and spoiled to enjoy her friends perhaps it would be better to just sit and listen to her hold forth on her own problem of rehabilitation. She could promote herself as a shining white example. Then, when she ran down, they could get up and walk on. "I suppose coming back here was quite a change," he said, to start her off.

Bitsy turned and gave him a long, level look. Her face was as blank as a page in her new notebook, and as closed. "I didn't mean to bore you," she said. "I was simply trying to tell you about myself so you'd stop feeling as if you're the only person in the world who has something to overcome. However, I'm sure that illness is much more difficult to recover from than a rotten disposition, so I probably could never understand you. I've apologized for being a snip, so now I'll go home."

She was angry to have humbled herself before anyone so rich and self-centered as Davy, and she flung her half-eaten apple away as if it had worms in it, and was about to pick up her books when he laid his hand on them. "I don't know how to ask you this, Bitsy," he said, "except to be blunt and come right out with it. Did you really come over to square things with me—or to do a good deed?"

"Does it matter?" Bitsy shrugged and looked off at his big, fancy home in the distance, as she said, "You *want* to feel sorry for yourself, so I was stupid to come."

"No, I don't, Bits." Davy considered his words, then sat staring at his legs again. "Well, maybe I do," he admitted. "Maybe I'm not so all-fired independent as I try to pretend I am. I told you I was tied up in knots."

"Why, Davy?" She stopped being angry and slid around to face him. His long slender hand still lay on top of her geometry book, and she wondered if tapping it would remind him to answer. But she waited.

David was having a struggle. He could tell Bitsy his secret and perhaps regret it, or he could let the moment pass and possibly regret that, too. Did he trust her? Did he like her? Or was he simply a little goony because he was sitting on a grassy bank beside a pretty girl in a blue denim skirt and blazer? He didn't know, and he sighed.

"Tell me, please tell me," she said softly. "What's wrong with you, Davy?"

"My leg," he muttered, as if the confession were being wrenched out of him. And he looked up to say hotly, "It's my darned, blasted leg!"

Bitsy's gaze didn't drop to his boots as he had expected it would; it stayed fixed on his face, and she said, "I don't quite understand. I've never noticed anything wrong with your leg."

"You've never seen it." Davy, having gone this far, was suddenly impatient to blurt the whole thing out. He did like Bitsy. He was sure of it now, so she might as well decide if she could like him in return or would turn away from him in disgust. "Why do you suppose I never swim when anybody's around?" he asked. "Or put on shorts? I can't, that's why."

"Why, Davy, of *course* you can." Bitsy's blue eyes were full of compassion as she said, "It's just a *leg!* What would you do if you had a scarred face? You couldn't hide it. So why should you want to hide one of your legs because it doesn't match the other one?"

"You haven't seen it," he answered. "It's repulsive."

"It wouldn't be to me." Bitsy shook her head at him and gave a soft, scolding click of her tongue. "Davy Parrish," she said, "I can't believe that any boy as good-looking as you are would be so conscious of an ugly leg. It doesn't *hurt* you, does it?"

"Not too much, but it's weak."

"It's strong enough to ride a horse," she pointed out.

"In a padded boot."

"And it gets you over fences." She smiled at him then and laid her hand over his, as she said, "I know it's awfully hard, Davy. I'm sure I should hate it, too—only I'd be mean and mad at everybody who was better off than I was. You've always wanted to go to West Point, haven't you?"

"When I was little I did. I've kissed that off."

"Then wipe it out of your mind."

She lifted her eyes to the sky that looked like a piece of blue silk stretched above them, wondering what she could say to comfort him. Last winter she had worried about choosing the right words to comfort Keith, and Ellin had told her she would find them. She had, but Keith was different from Davy. He was well and whole and had a future, even if he couldn't put Susan in it. Perhaps this case needed action rather than words.

"I'm not a doctor," she said, "so I don't know about ligaments and bones and things, but I think you had better take off your boot and show me your leg."

Davy jerked back. No one but Lang and the doctors had seen his deformity since he was twelve years old; and Lang had seen it only because he had blundered into Davy's room without knocking first. "Some other time," he said.

"Then I wish it were summer." Bitsy was disappointed but she wouldn't argue. "When it is," she said, "I'll make you swim in the pool with me. And after what you've told me, you'll have to, or be chicken. And I'll expect you to go hiking with me in shorts, and to get used to having me seeing your leg. I'm very determined."

Only silence answered her, so she ordered

crossly, "Oh, stop bottling it up, Davy. Your family ought to look at you, too, and all your friends. Good heavens," she said, staring straight at him, "how do you ever expect to get married?"

"I don't." Davy had to grin at her straightforwardness. "I'm resigned to that," he said; and she clicked her tongue again.

She had no desire to look at his leg, now, but she did worry about his mental block. It's often wise to put cotton batting around a sore leg but a sick mind should never be wrapped up. She didn't know how she knew that, but she did, and she said, "Now that I know what your problem is we can be better friends. I didn't learn to dance until last winter because I thought *I* had a problem, and you can jolly well learn now. You can dance, and you can swim, and I do *not* intend to put my hands over my eyes while you go sneaking into the water. Shame on you, Davy Parrish," she scolded, warming to her task. "You're such a wonderful boy that I don't see how you could be so sensitive and foolish. Will you stop it?"

"Sure. I'll try."

"As of this minute." She leaned over and gave his boot a pat. "Isn't it nice, Davy," she asked, looking around at him, her voice suddenly light and gay, "that we know each other so well?"

"It's swell," he answered, feeling like Pilgrim when his burden dropped from his shoulders. He *would* swim with Bitsy, by golly, and perhaps with Lang and Vance, and even his parents. As Bitsy had said, what was a mismatched leg?

They sat talking while the blue silk sky changed to rainbow gauze, and when they walked on along the lane again, he was carrying Bitsy's books and promising to explain to Susan that Bitsy's tardiness had been his fault.

CHAPTER 8

PARRI WAS SITTING ON THE TOP STEP of the terrace when Bitsy and Davy crossed the driveway. Her brown head with a big red bow behind each ear was bent over her starchy plaid lap and she stared down at her two hands that for once were still.

"Hi, punk," Davy called, and she looked up.

"Oh, hi." Then she raised her left hand that had something sparkling on a finger and said airily, "Isn't this a beautiful ring?"

"Handsome." From a distance, a cluster of rubies and diamonds glittered magnificently, but when Davy laid Bitsy's books on the step and bent over for closer inspection he saw that the stones weren't real and that gleaming platinum was only white metal. "How much of your allowance did that cost you?" he asked.

"Oh, it didn't cost me anything," Parri answered, flashing her hand about. "Carlton Aikens bought it for me. We're engaged."

"Engaged!" Davy looked inquiringly at Bitsy, but her face was as blank as his.

"It's the style," Parri explained. "Practically every girl in my room is engaged, but they just have dime-store rings. Carlton spent a dollar and twenty-nine cents for mine. He wanted me to have the best. It was very thoughtful of him, don't you think?"

Neither Bitsy nor Davy answered her. They were too busy staring at her in puzzled surprise, so she went on to clarify a situation that every girl and boy in the sixth grade understood, or even in the fifth, and the fourth. "You can't go steady with a boy unless he gives you a ring. It wouldn't look right."

"Do you go steady?" Davy found his voice to ask.

"Of course." Her red bows nodded proudly, but he only frowned as if he were even more puzzled.

"When?" he asked.

Parri and Joshu had been enrolled in the fine new glass-and-brick public school in the village, and for eight school days a county school bus had taken them there and delivered them home again. Except for playtime and lunchtime, there was no time for girl-and-boy business, and he couldn't see how Parri and this Carlton kid could go steady in play yards that were on opposite sides of the school, or in a crowded cafeteria.

"Why, whenever we get a chance," Parri answered simply. "At least I don't go with any *other* boy. And whenever we have school parties, I'll dance every dance with him, and there'll be a children's party at Christmas, and then there's the Scouts' football game. Carlton's trying awfully hard to make the team so I can sit in the bleachers and cheer for him. We have lots of time to go steady."

"Can you beat it?" Davy looked at Bitsy, who shook her head. Then they both looked at Parri again, and Davy said, "Your mother'll have a fit."

"Oh, she'll murder me." Parri grinned cheerfully and unclasped a gold chain from around her neck. "Carlton paid an extra quarter for this," she said. "It's the style, too, and you wear your ring on it so the teachers won't see it. And parents, too," she added, "although Mums has awfully eagle-ish eyes."

The door behind her opened, and as Penny and Tippy came out, she murmured, "Oh—oh. Are you going to tell her?"

"You bet."

Davy thought it only fair to let his aunts finish whatever they were saying to Susan who was still inside before he blew up a storm, but Parri hopped up from the step and waved her jeweled hand at them.

"Look, Mums," she said. "Look at what Carlton gave me."

"Uhhuh." Penny was not ignorant of this silly fad that had been sweeping through the lower grades for the past year but she didn't see how Parri could have got coupled to someone so quickly, not in just eight days. She must be a fast worker.

"It's pretty," was all she said. "If you're going to wear an engagement ring you ought to learn which finger it belongs on. The fourth, not the middle finger, is the right one."

"It's a little too big for that one."

Parri was about to change the ring, but her mother sighed. "Poor Carlton, whoever he is," she said pityingly. "He must have spent a lot of good money on you."

"He pried his bank open," Parri said proudly, "and took all his life's savings."

"And what are you planning to do for him?" Parri didn't see Penny wink, but the others did, before she went on, "Engagements aren't one-sided, you know. What do you plan to do for Carlton?"

"Why—why, I'm going to dance with him," Parri answered uncertainly. "I'm going to give him all my spare time. Isn't that enough?"

"Not for most boys."

Penny shook her head and looked doubtful. She wasn't reacting as Parri had expected her to, nor as any of the others thought the seriousness of the situation demanded. The two in high school thought she should give the pert young piece a good blast; and Tippy, mother of a daughter not yet two, was sure she would handle the situation with a much firmer hand.

"Engagements are a two-way stretch," Penny said, looking thoughtful. "If you're engaged to Carlton, you'll have to stop playing with the Carter boys down the road. Also, it will mean that you'll have to stop helping Joshu's gang build the dam in the brook," she decreed as Parri's mouth opened in protest. "And you'll have to stay home when Daddy takes Lang and his friends on the tour of Radio City and to watch the new musical from backstage. As for your birthday party," she shrugged and said matter-of-factly, "we'll talk it over later, Parri. I don't seem to remember any Carlton on your list."

"I don't know where he lives," Parri confessed unhappily. "Way over in some other direction, I think. But maybe his mother could bring him."

"Perhaps. If she can't we'll cancel the party. We'll talk it over with Daddy."

"But, Mums!" Parri could see long lonely afternoons ahead. Going steady was fine at school but it didn't work at home. Not if you got yourself engaged to someone who lived miles and miles away. She liked the Carter twins better than Carlton, but neither twin would spend so much as a nickel on her, let alone buy her a ring that had a luxury tax added on. "High school kids go steady and have rings," she explained, both to justify what seemed a little silly now and to strengthen her case. "We're only trying to copy what they do."

"Then go ahead and copy them, you foolish little thing," Penny answered, remembering the fun she had had at Parri's age with her gang. Then she sighed. Poor little Parri was growing up in a different age from hers. Childish engagements, space travel, missile rockets, hurry, hurry, hurry. Get engaged at eleven so you'll be sure to have some of this earth's experiences before your parents decide to pick up and go live on Venus.

"This business wasn't my idea," she said, knowing that everyone was waiting for her to make Parri take off that ridiculous ring, "but I'll do my best to keep you true to the poor kid who robbed a bank for you."

"But I don't think I want to be engaged now," Parri said, twisting the gaudy ring that had seemed so gorgeous a few minutes before. "I'd rather build the dam and go on the trip to New York. I'll tell Carlton so and give him back his ring."

"Wup, wait a minute. Do you have the money it cost to give back with it?" Penny asked, hearing Tippy's breath come out in a relieved sigh. "You'll have to pay Carlton back to be fair," she went on, wanting to bend over and kiss the white part on Parri's brown head, but explaining carefully, "because it was such a short engagement. No other girl will want to take a secondhand ring. And no borrowing from Joshu," she decreed, knowing what a free spender Parri was, while Joshu hoarded his allowance to buy something big that he really wanted.

"Do you mean I'll have to stay engaged to Carlton for three weeks?" Parri asked, lifting miserable brown eyes. "It'll take me that long to save enough, and I'll have missed—everything."

Davy put his hand in his pocket but Penny shook her head at him. "You're the one who'll have to work it out, honey," she said. "You may like being engaged by the time you can pay your way out, so you'd better wait and see."

Parri took off the ring that didn't seem so sparkly now. "I won't," she said, holding it out. "Maybe you'd better keep this until I get home and can find its box. It did come in a lovely box, and I think I know where I put it. Here."

"Heavens, no." Penny backed away and put her hands behind her. "I might lose it," she said, "and I don't want to be responsible for it. Put it on again, it's safer that way."

"All right." Parri slipped the ring back on, flinging her head up in a gesture so like her mother's that Tippy couldn't keep from smiling. "I got my stupid self into this so I'll get my stupid self out," she said. And she marched down the steps.

"Nice going," Davy commented as Penny passed him. "Think you can do as well when your time comes, Aunt Tip?"

"Let's hope the craze will have passed by then," Tippy answered. "Although if it has there'll be something else to worry about. Have you given out any rings yet?"

"Not in my school. We aren't a mixed group."

Davy grinned and looked at Bitsy. "How about you?" he asked.

"No, thanks." Bitsy remembered seeing heavy signet and class rings decorating the engagement fingers of some of her schoolmates, but until today she had never thought much about it.

"It's a queer custom to have started," she said, her eyes following Parri as she skipped along toward Gladstone between Penny and Carrol. "Even the original business of engagement rings. It's a public announcement of honorable intentions between a man and a woman, I suppose—the giving, the accepting—and every girl is proud of hers. But imagine having had five or six before the real time comes! Why, it would be like saying thank you for a box of candy."

She turned to find David watching her, his eyes quizzical, yet his mouth twitching against a smile, and she said quickly, "Oh, I know I'm rather old-fashioned. It's just that I get a terrific boot out of firsts—first long formal, first orchid, first fraternity pin or class ring. Fraternity pins aren't as binding as a diamond, but I don't even want one of those until I'm really serious."

"Count me in for the same." Davy picked up her books again and handed them to her, then said as she stood hugging them, "You're okay, Bitsy. Thanks for a swell afternoon."

"Let's have more, Davy," she answered impulsively. "Come over whenever you care to, and don't forget that you promised not to be so stupidly sensitive about your leg. It's a perfectly good leg," she said, seeing his shoulders stiffen, "and you'll simply have to learn to be grateful. And I want to tell you something else," she added, leaning a little closer to him. "Even if you had two good legs that matched, you couldn't be exactly like your father."

"Who says I want to be?"

"You do. Everything about you says it. I'd like to be as wonderful as Susan, too," she pointed out, "but I can't. I'm Bitsy and you're Davy, so let's make the most of ourselves. I rather like us as we are."

"I'll learn to." Davy gave her a pat between her shoulder blades as he swung away, then called back in a teasing voice which surprised him as much as it did her, "I've got a swell ring that I made out of wire and a bullet when I was eight. How about sending it over?"

"In a box," she called back, laughing. "Don't forget the box—and giftwrap it."

He waved assent as he went on; and as she went up the steps Susan came to the door again. "What's so funny?" Susan asked. "Parri? I had to miss the end of the session. Did Penny straighten her out?"

"Beautifully. Penny's smarter than I'd ever be. I wanted to slap the silly little thing."

Bitsy skipped up the steps, and Susan said, "Tell me all about it later. Rosie's here, and I've got her settled in the sewing room. As Bobby would say, 'she flew right up on her little fairy wings,' and she looks awfully permanent."

"I can oust her when it's time." Bitsy felt very efficient. Hadn't she pumped courage into Davy? Hadn't she restored Keith's faith in himself? Most of Keith's restoration had happened in her dreams, of course, but she had put some of it into practice yesterday, and now she would begin working on a dream for Davy. "I'll take care of Rosie after you're gone," she promised gaily, dusting off her books that had bits of grass and gravel on them from such an up-and-down afternoon, and plopping them on the table where Plush had arranged himself for a nap. "Where is the happy moron?"

"In the kitchen by now, I think, because Ellin has stopped singing." Susan led the way through the dining room, whispering as they went, "I had to send Bobby to meet her in the village, because Penny and Tippy were here, you know, and by the time he got home with her you'd have thought that Rosie was the bride. Bobby assisted her out of the car a lot more gallantly than he ever has me, and lugged in her suitcase that was not only locked but bound around and around with rope. He paid her so many compliments, too, that she got the giggles and knocked her hat off. He was wonderful, and he made her think we couldn't do without her."

"Poor Rosie," Bitsy whispered back. "She isn't much older than Jenifer, and she's never had any fun."

"Well, she's having a ball now." Susan pushed

open the kitchen door and watched Bitsy be as magnificent as Bobby had.

"*Rosie!*" Bitsy cried, scarcely remembering the startling figure that jumped up and held her at arm's length. And looking at the bright pink cheeks and wild black hair that stuck out around a frilly white maid's cap, she added, "Why, you haven't changed at all."

"My goodness, but *you* have!" Rosie exclaimed. "You've grown, you pretty little thing. You've grown a lot more than Susan. Has Vance grown too?"

"He should have, if he isn't a dwarf." Bitsy wondered why the cap. It was probably something Rosie had seen a parlormaid wear in a movie, but straight on her head, not all crooked; and she tried to pull her eyes down from it.

"I always wore one of these on Governors Island, remember?" Rosie said, seeing Bitsy's stare and touching the yellowed band tenderly. "Ellin made me."

And at her words Bitsy's whole small childhood with her family came flooding back. There was Rosie, tying down her flying hair and passing out dozens and dozens of cookies to little people who lovingly followed her around. There was Ellin, calm, serene, bandaging skinned knees, tucking in covers, comforting and dear.

"Oh, Rosie," she cried, in a glad remembering rush, "I'm so glad you're home again! I don't know how we can ever let you go!"

Now she'd done it! Susan told her so in no uncertain terms when they were back in the living room and Bitsy was still a little dazed from her own impetuous reception of an old-time servant. "She'll never want to leave now," Susan ended.

"I know it." The past was beginning to separate itself from the present. The feeling that all this was as it had used to be—the kitchen, Rosie's tender arms around her—was slowly fading. She wasn't the baby Bitsy. "I'm sorry," she said. "I didn't know something strange would happen to me when I saw Rosie. It all came back so suddenly, but I'll fix it."

"I hope you can." Susan walked to the door and said, looking out, "Without hurting her, I mean. We don't need her, Bitsy, and Daddy can't afford to keep her. You've made her think she's going to stay."

"I've said I'm sorry." To be impulsive was not one of Bitsy's many faults. She felt unreasoning resentment because Susan couldn't see it, but she only said, "The past popped back, that's all. It was so real it frightens me. I'll get rid of her, Susan, truly I will."

"Poor baby." Susan showed she did understand after all. "We all took a beating," she said, "Rosie with us, and even Ellin for a time. But that was long ago. Rosie was young then and should have made a life for herself."

"I'll explain everything to her."

The sun was low in the sky and a faint hazy pink glow spread over the world outside as Bitsy walked slowly up the stairway and stopped at a small window set in the circular tower. It's beautiful and strange, she thought, looking out. But then, everything has been rather strange today.

CHAPTER 9

"THE BUCKET AND MOP BRIGADE has arrived," Tippy called up the stairway to Susan, the next morning. "We charge by the hour, portal to portal, so you'd better hurry."

"Coming."

Susan could be heard running along the hall, so Tippy went back to the living room where Penny and Carrol waited. The three had offered to give the small apartment above the garage a thorough cleaning, and they looked crisply efficient in shirts and shorts: the lovely Carrol in pink, Tippy in light blue, and Penny in tan linen. Carrol had planned to quietly send her own staff from Gladstone, and to freshen up the apartment with inexpensive slip covers, but Penny, with a reluctant Tippy for an ally, had voted her down.

"This will be fun," Penny had argued, looking

eager and almost as young as Tippy, in spite of the ten years' difference in their ages. "You don't realize how seldom I get to be with a bunch of girls. Even if we louse everything up and streak the walls, it will be a ball for me. I'm 'between engagements,' as we say in the theater, so let's have at it. I'll bring the lunch, and my own mop and pail."

So here they were, two of them completely inexperienced in housework, and one who was enjoying her vacation from it. Tippy, after four years of marriage, was sure she had washed enough dishes to outline the Turnpike from New York to Pittsburgh, and had made more beds and dusted more furniture every year than any maid in a big hotel. "Oh, no," she had protested faintly, but neither her sister nor her sister-in-law had listened to her.

"It's going to be fun," they had promised, and she doubtingly hoped it would be.

Susan looked cute, if not bridelike, when she came down. Her red-flowered Hawaiian shirt hung loosely over a pair of very faded red shorts and her long legs ended in the old tennis shoes she wore to wash the cars whenever Vance forgot to.

"Where's Bobby?" Tippy asked, thinking that a bride without lipstick and with her hair covered by a brown scarf wasn't exactly what a groom would swoon over so early in the morning.

"Oh, he's going over the books with Mr. Whitlaw," Susan answered. "He'll be right underneath us but he has to work. He can't come up and it's about to kill him. Bobby doesn't know a piston from a flat tire," she said, shrugging, "so he's planning to learn in three easy lessons. He does know," she added, defending him, "when a four-door car is more practical than a two, and when a family should buy a station wagon instead of a convertible, but he hasn't the least idea what's in the stock of parts that he signed for. Robert," she promised, "won't be up to bother us. Shall we start?"

She felt very important when they climbed out of Carrol's long station wagon that took up all the reserved space beside Parrish Motors, Inc., and put her fine new key in the lock of a door. The sidewalk behind her was piled with mops, brooms, pails, and large cardboard cartons containing cleaning rags and detergents, and she took her share of them as they climbed a steep inside stairway. "This is it," she said, shifting her burden so she could fit another key into another door that had a grimy pane of glass in it. "Welcome to Parrish Manor."

Penny and Carrol had been in the apartment before but Tippy looked at the small living room with a cluttered kitchen at one end, partly concealed like a blot on the décor by a low plywood wall, and said "Ugh. It's even worse than I had at Fort Knox when Peter was a student."

"Both only temporary," Susan retorted smugly, pulling up a rackety Venetian blind that left most of its slats hanging crooked. "When we get everything clean and move the furniture around it won't look so bad. Bobby and I think it's keen. It's ours, at least, and snug, which our fine house isn't yet."

Another blind refused to rise when she tugged at it, so she left it sagging like a concertina with its air out, and hauled one of the boxes around to look into it. "What do you suggest we use?" she asked.

"Everything the TV commercials recommend," Carrol answered, burrowing down with her. "I've brought them all. If one doesn't do the job we can try a second coat with something else. Perkins said these are for the floor," she said, setting out an array of bottles and tins of wax. "Everything else is for walls and furniture except these, and they're for dishes and pans."

"You don't happen to have an electric dishwasher, do you?" Tippy asked hopefully, thinking of all those miles and miles of dishes she had washed; and the others jeered.

"Fall to, men," Penny commanded, having already chosen what she needed. "I'm starting on the living-room walls and I may slosh, so keep out of my way."

Carrol went off to the small dark bedroom and Susan to the rust-stained bathroom beyond, so Tippy drew the kitchen, just as she had been almost sure she would.

For a whole hour there was only the sound of water gushing as pails were filled, of steel wool scraping, of the swish of brushes on stubborn paint that hated to part with its grime, then Penny started walking about on an inspection tour. The rooms looked clean. They smelled clean, too, with a dozen different scents that a dozen different chemical firms had added to their products in a last all-out promotion to attract the sensitive noses of the women who would have to use them.

"Coffee break!" she suddenly called, having elected herself foreman of the gang. "Come on, everyone, let's take a coffee break."

"Sh!" Tippy shot out of the bathroom where she had gone to help Susan fight the rust stains. "Bobby'll hear you," she whispered, listening. "He's got the ears of a fox, and if he thinks we're stopping to have fun he won't care how many nuts and bolts he's left uncounted. He'll race right up."

Brushes were laid down gently, not dropped, and feet began to move on tiptoe toward the picnic basket. Penny even unscrewed the top on the thermos bottle as if it might squeak and betray them through a double thickness of floor, but Carrol said, "Oh, pooh. All we have to do is lock the door. He can't see through the glass because we haven't washed it." And she asked, "Don't we want him?"

"Not till we've finished work." Tippy had lived through a whole year and a half of Bobby at Fort Knox. He had had the happy faculty of turning up whenever she was busiest, and she said knowingly, "He'll only slow us down. I'm having fun, but I do have a baby at home that I can't leave with Mums and Trudy too long, and Peter gets lonely without me. If Bobby comes up and starts clowning around we'll never finish."

"How right you are." Penny, too, had grown up with Bobby. And while she had seen him less frequently since her marriage than Tippy had, she stopped prying up the lid on a tin of cookies and jumped up to lock the door.

Only Carrol remembered that Susan would be marrying Bobby in four days so might like to be with him, and suggested in her sweet, quiet way, "I think we should ask him up to lunch."

"He can't come." Susan smiled gratefully at her, and said, "Mr. Whitlaw is taking him to the Businessmen's Club for lunch. He thinks Bobby should join it. I told you he couldn't come up."

"Hooray." Penny finished taking the lid off the box of cookies and passed it around.

The morning work progressed, lunch was eaten around a clean table on four clean white chairs, and when three o'clock came what remained of the detergents was put away under the kitchen sink and a box of trash set outside on a high back porch.

"Sure we can't give you a lift home, Susan?" Penny asked, the last to wash, scrubbing her hands and using a paper towel to wipe out the sink again.

"No, thanks. Bobby's going to drive me up to see Neal and I said I'd wait for him here. I've been neglecting Neal shamefully this last week," she explained, "and since he can't come home till Friday night, Bobby said he would drive up to the Point and be back by the time Alcie and Jon get here."

"We'll be over to see Alcie tonight," Tippy said. "She's still my best friend, and now that she's going to have a baby at last, we'll have such loads to get off in a corner and talk, talk, talk about." Then she scowled at the chipped dishes in the cupboards and suggested, as she had wanted to do all the time she had been washing them, "You really ought to bring over your good china, Susan. This stuff is *awful!*"

"I'll talk to Bobby about it, and we may buy a cheap set. We want to keep everything new for our own house," Susan explained. "At least I do," she said. "Bobby won't care. And oh, I do thank you for helping me. I'd really dreaded doing it and didn't see where I'd ever get the time, and now here it is, shining clean. I can devote all day tomorrow to getting ready for our party tomorrow night without worrying about it, and I just may be able to finish up all the hundred and one things I still have to do if I'm to get to the church on time."

"Anything left that we can take care of?" Penny asked, handing Carrol her pail and mop, and keeping her own and the brooms.

"No, I don't think so, thanks. I have to pick up my wedding dress and veil in New York on Thursday and rush over to the photographer's with them for the photographs Daddy wants. It's going to take a chunk out of my day," she sighed, "but Daddy wants a picture to frame with Jenifer's and Alcie's, so I'll have to do it. And Friday? Oh, murder!"

She spread her hands helplessly, and the other three who had known the day-before-my-wedding excitement nodded understandingly. Each remembered her own: Penny the rush of added Christmas shopping; Carrol the sadness of her father's death; and Tippy the last-minute confusion of squeezing a little Jordon in as one of her bridesmaids because she was so lonely and abandoned. Her mother had dropped everything to make a flowered wreath for Susan's hair, she remembered, and Susan had walked proudly back along the aisle beside the youngest groomsman, Bobby. It all seemed such a short time ago, with the intervening years while Susan was growing up and would have none of Bobby simply flying by. And now here was Susan, supposedly in full control of her senses, yet promising to love, cherish, and honor the idiot.

"I wish you were going to live at Knox, near Peter and me," she stayed behind to say when the other two were clanking down the stairway. "Peter has so much sense."

And at that Susan burst into laughter. Tippy's little face was so puckered with loving worry and her amber eyes said as plainly as if they had spoken aloud, "I don't want you to have Bobby walking all over you again and making you miserable."

"Look, Tippy dear," she said when she could, and still smiling. "Robert and I aren't going to walk into that church on Saturday afternoon as two separate individuals and come out as one—with the *one* having the whip hand. We'll still be two people. We'll be loving each other and united in a long, long future, but . . . well, you didn't see Bobby in Hong Kong," she said, the smile fading in her pride. "I did. I know his capabilities. I know all about his charm, his little-boy willfulness, his determination to have his own way, but I found out that he's a fine man, too, a man I can lean on in a crisis. You probably won't believe it, Tip, but he's wonderful."

"I'm glad, darling." Tippy put her arm around Susan and said sincerely, "I just wanted to be sure you're happy. Sometimes families are too close to really see each other, so perhaps I have a wrong picture of Bobby." A long blast on a horn made her pick up her pail and say hastily, "I've loved you a long time, Susy, you know, and somehow my closeness to Alcie got transferred to you. You grew into her place."

"The same as I did with Bobby." Susan grinned understandingly and watched Tippy go running down the steep stairway, her pail banging against the wall.

She loved all the Parrishes—her Aunt Marjorie and Uncle Dave, almost as much as her own father, then Tippy and all the others down the line. They would be nearby to love her in return, but not to hamper her. They would leave her free to love Bobby most of all, and to work out their own life together in this dear, funny apartment.

She closed the door, liking the cozy click it gave, and walked about with her hands clasped behind her. She felt like whistling. She and Neal had always whistled together when they were happy, sometimes arias from operas, sometimes popular songs, and sometimes bugle calls to wake the rest of the family. Dear Neal. She would miss him so terribly. She and Bobby would be happy together in a strange new world of their own, so she decided to whistle now, for Neal. Flutelike notes filled the air, and she was so happy just sending them out that she didn't hear footsteps on the stairway. Then the door opened and Bobby came in.

"Lord help us," he said, "I thought you'd gone and bought a canary. When did you learn to do all that?"

"When I was a twin." She broke off on a high note and put her arms around the shoulders of his wilted new fall suit. "I whistled all the time the winter I lived at your house," she said, looking up into his eyes, "but you didn't have time to notice my musical, girlish pipings. Aren't you a little dressed up for such a warm day?"

"Gosh, yes." Bobby held her off and frowned at her. "I used to hear you whistling around like a happy little nightingale," he said, "but I didn't know I was going to fall for the mating call. Look what it's done to me. I'm darn near melted."

"And I haven't even an ice cube to offer you." Susan laid her cheek against his necktie that felt hot and body-damp, and asked, "Was it very bad?"

"It was swell. You know," he said, pulling her over a waxed space to the sofa, "I felt like a real businessman. I truly did."

"Eeeek!" Susan jerked back and left him bent over like a jockey giving his horse the whip at the finish line. "Don't *sit!*" she shrieked. "The cushions are wet. They had spots on them and we washed them!"

"Now you tell me." Caught off balance he went on down but bounced promptly up again. "Is that wet, too?" he asked, pointing to a chair that looked as if it had held two people many a time, possibly three or four if the occupants were small; and she nodded.

"Everything's wet," she said. "And the rug's so wet that it's hanging over the back porch railing."

"What's in the rest of the dump?"

Tippy would have thought him callous, but Susan didn't. Tippy would have said that the big clown didn't appreciate all the work and effort she had put into making a grubby apartment habitable for him, and would have expected him to put his arms around her and praise her the way Peter surely would. Susan only said, "Nothing much," and led him on a tour.

"You mean we sleep on *those?*" Bobby asked, looking only at two lumpy beds when she showed him a shining clean bedroom. "Not me. Where are the ones with the great big double-job headboard the folks gave us?"

"We both agreed that we don't want to use those, Bobby."

"Then buy some more."

He was being very grand, Susan thought, for an Army lieutenant who had resigned with only his last month's pay in the bank. "Yes, sir," she said. "Now, if you'll sit down on the floor and write me a check . . ."

"Oh, Daffy-dilly." Bobby's arms went around her and he kissed her under her soft round chin. "My dear Daffy-dilly," he whispered, feeling the beat of her heart pulsing against his lips, "I'll sleep on the floor, I'll eat out of a tin pan, I'll count stock and sell gas till I'm groggy, as long as you're going to be my wife. I'm not much to marry, but please do it."

"We're sending over some extra mattresses from Carrol's," Susan told him, wishing they never had to move. "And we're taking one of our smaller wedding checks to buy some decent china because our future tenants will need it later. Stop getting so excited, darling."

"I want you to have the best."

Bobby forgot that he was the one who had objected to the discomfort of lumpy beds, and by the time they had locked the door on their small domain, was proclaiming it a veritable palace. "Gosh, just two days to wait," he said happily, as he put Susan into the inexpensive demonstrator sedan that he had exchanged his rakish convertible for. "Did you see the new sign?"

"I admired it," she answered, "proudly and silently—so your sisters wouldn't think I was too impressed before I had a right to be—and I loved it. Do you think I look good enough to talk to Neal, if I don't get out of the car?"

"If you take that awful thing off your head, you do," he answered, fussing about with unfamiliar gadgets. "You might frighten Neal."

Susan untied her scarf and reached up to pull down the sunshade on her side of the windshield, to look into the mirror clipped to its underside. But there was no mirror. Instead, there was a neat leather case that matched the gray upholstery, and the case was fitted with a comb, a shiny new compact exactly like the one she always used, a lipstick, a coin purse, and a package of Bobby's favorite cigarettes.

"We stock them," Bobby said, when she gave a little gasp of pleasure. "I took one out of a box, and I'll have you know I charged it to myself—very honorably. I rang it up on the cash register and it was my first sale, all but the compact and the lipstick. I gave Bitsy the money to buy those. Look in the coin purse."

Susan reached up to inspect each item, and when she opened the flat leather envelope, two dimes and three nickels fell into her hand. "For parking meters and tolls," he said grandly. "I'm the kind of husband who thinks of every little detail."

"You're absolutely wonderful!" Susan used the comb and tried the lipstick, then leaned over and left the print of her lips on Bobby's cheek. "My first present from you," she said softly; and at that Bobby let out one of his familiar yells.

"What do you mean, your first present?" he demanded. "What about all the stuff I've been cluttering you up with for years? Flowers, candy, the basket of fruit I bought for your trip to the Orient—and the Mikimoto pearls I hocked my pay for in Japan. Those pearls were . . ."

"The gift of the groom. I know. That's what you kept telling me when you gave them to me. But you see, darling," Susan said tenderly, "I didn't dream that you were going to be my groom then, so that's why I had to give them back. Do you know what I'm going to do with them now?"

"No, what?" Bobby had seen the soft creamy choker around Susan's neck for the last week, but he waited to hear her quote him as he had quoted from wedding writeups in newspapers:

" 'The bride wore pearls, the gift of the groom.' I'm going to wear mine for my something new, and I have a little turquoise heart that belonged to Mother. I'll pin it on somewhere."

"I think," Bobby said, considering, "that I'll borrow a new handkerchief from Dad and stick a piece of Mum's blue stationery in my pocket and wear a pair of my old socks. Say," he turned his head to ask, "why can't the groom have fun being superstitious, the way the bride does?"

"He has every right to be, and you just be it."

"By gum, I'm going to. It's half my wedding and I'm not going to hide around in corners while everybody makes a fuss over the bride. I'll have my nice new ring, and I'll be wearing my nice blue uniform that looked good enough to dance with the President's cousin, and I'll smell of after-shave lotion, and my hair will be set in pretty waves. . . ."

"Oh, Bobby!" Susan bent over and giggles came up from her lap. "You make the wedding sound like fun," she said. And she peeked up at him and threatened, "But if you start me laughing in the middle of it I'll walk right smack out of the church. You won't even get your nice new ring."

"Oh, I'll be so good," he promised, hauling her up where he could look at her. "But I won't be any walking ghost like Peter and David and Josh were. Peter almost shook himself loose from his shoes while we were waiting for Tippy to get down the aisle, but I don't intend to. If you take too long about it I'll walk right up and get you."

"You wouldn't!" Susan's eyes were as round as blue china plates because she feared that that was exactly what he might take a notion to do. If the notion struck him his brain would telegraph his feet and they would start moving. It was almost a relief to hear him promise:

"I said I'd be good, Daffy-dilly, but it might

be wise for you to hustle along in march time."

"I can't hustle Alcie and Bitsy and Parri," she reminded.

"Then pass 'em on the way or give 'em a poke."

Susan had to laugh at the picture of a bridal party going along the aisle, each one prodding the one ahead, but he said, "You know something? I've got an idea. You wanted this to be a strictly family wedding, except for my roommate at the Point and the guy who's flying out from Knox to usher, but how about taking one of them out of the line-up and putting Keith in?"

"But it's to be a *military* wedding!" Susan cried. "You're the one who insisted on having Stretch Jackson and Tony Carstairs so they could hold up enough sabers for us to walk under."

"I wouldn't mind skipping that. I got to thinking about poor old Keith. . . ."

"Bobby, you're sweet." Susan laid her hand over his on the wheel and looked at him with her eyes shining. She understood the tussle he must have had with himself, the complete capitulation and going overboard that always followed his spells of selfishness. Bobby never could walk straight along a road. He zigzagged from far left to far right, following a drunken course that took him much longer than any sensible person; but if he ever did arrive at his destination, and he usually did, he had had an interesting trip along the way.

"We don't want Keith, darling, we really don't," she said, "and he doesn't want us. But thank you for suggesting it. You can ask him if you want to," she added, not wanting to spoil such a magnanimous gesture, "but I'm sure he'll refuse." And she thought confidently, Alcie will see that he does.

"Sure, I'll ask him."

They were passing through the wide gateway to West Point; and watching the easy way in which Bobby returned the salute of the guard who stepped out of his sentry box, she said, "It must seem strange to you to come back here this way, out of uniform."

"I had four swell years," he answered, wishing he were sweeping along the roadway past the Thayer Hotel in his ex-Cadillac. "As Parri would say, 'They were strictly from Keenville.'"

Then he gave an unconscious sigh. Cadets, or more often their fathers, didn't buy Cadillacs at graduation time. Only the old grads, the colonels and the brigadier generals, parked their Cadillacs in front of the Officers Club. This neat little model he was driving, and the compact car he planned to add to his line, were the kind that would buy the meat and potatoes for his and Susan's daily living. "Isn't that Neal standing out in front of Grant Hall?" he asked.

"Oh, it is." Susan had the door unlatched and was ready to leap from the car before it had quite stopped, then remembered her shorts and bare legs. "Oh, hi!" she called, thinking how handsome Neal looked, crossing the street.

He wore his full-dress uniform, the one he

would wear for her wedding, his tall shako topped with a waving black captain's plume, his white gloves swinging with the precision of his military stride. "What made you so late?" he asked, closing the door to lean on it, and scowling at them. "I've got parade in ten minutes."

"We were detained," Susan said, with her face so close to his that she blocked Bobby out. "Oh, Neal, can't you come home before Friday? I want so much to talk to you."

"Not a chance." He pushed one white fingertip against her nose and said, "Stop stewing, twin. We'll have our heart-to-heart after the wedding rehearsal. I'm not going to let you marry another cadet without a lot of advice. Okay?" Then he managed to peer around her and say, "Hi, Bob. Take her home and explain to her that I've got to make formation. You've been through it."

"She doesn't understand the ways of the Army," Bobby said with a shrug. "She doesn't like them either. Look what happened to me."

He ruffled Susan's neatly combed curls to show her he had meant no malice; so she said dutifully, "You fiend," and leaned farther out to look searchingly at Neal. "I'm sorry we were so late," she said, her gaze focused on his like the lens of a camera, photographing a picture of his dear face that she could always keep. "We'll come and get you Friday, right after classes," she added. "And, Neal?"

"Yeah?"

"Nothing." She knew he had to go. The Army

always had to go. Women, love, home, children, nothing mattered when the Army was on the go, go, go. "We'll see you Friday," she said, remembering the years when she had said to her father, "We'll see you after the war," "after Korea," "after Turkey," "after Japan." And she was surprised when he snatched off his shako so he could shove his head inside and kiss her.

"So long until Friday," he called, and went loping off.

He looked so handsome and dear crossing the street. He was a half of herself that but for a freak accident of nature might have been all Neal or all Susan. "Oh, dear," she said, falling back. And for the first time in all her life she murmured, "It's so darned hard to be born a twin."

CHAPTER
10

"HONEY," ALICE SAID, lying on the sofa and looking at Susan who sat at a card table, snatching a few minutes to catch up on the courteous thanking of people for their wedding gifts, "I hate to say this, but I'm afraid I'll have to."

"Say what?" Susan asked, her forehead still puckered from hunting a new way to write *We're going to find so many, many uses for the beautiful tray you sent us,* because it was the tenth tray she had written about. What could one do with ten beautiful trays? "What?" she asked again, when Alice hadn't answered.

"I don't see how I can possibly be your matron of honor," Alice said, praying that the dizziness and nausea would pass enough for her to sit up until the family buffet supper was over. "I never know when I might suddenly woops, so what if I should . . ." Nausea seized her, and only by closing her eyes and lying still could she control it. "Ugh," she moaned.

"Oh, Alcie." Susan sprang up, scattering monogrammed notepaper and envelopes on the floor. "Sometimes you feel better," she said, kneeling by the sofa and taking Alice's limp hand in hers. "Last night you talked to Tippy and Peter all evening, and felt fine."

"But not now. Perhaps it's excitement, or standing up," Alice suggested, clutching her stomach. "But whatever it is, this darn baby gets mad the minute I move and starts churning around. I'm afraid to ruin your wedding, darling. Think how awful it would look if the matron of honor should suddenly whirl around and run out of the church."

The picture of Alice crowding past the startled bride and her father was amusing to Susan, but she sat down on the floor beside the sofa and asked seriously, "Don't you really think you can do it, Alcie?"

"Oh, golly, I don't see how." Alice was so wretched that she could only wish herself home in her own bed, or, at the very least, upstairs in one of Bitsy's. There was the party tonight to get through, the formal dinner at Carrol and David's, the wedding rehearsal. "Oh," she moaned.

"But there's your beautiful dress," Susan pointed out, "your beautiful bronze-colored dress that's almost like the one you wore in Jenifer's wedding, and was so expensive."

"Maybe you can find someone else who can wear it," Alice suggested, not caring if she came to the wedding in her bathrobe, if only Jonathan could get her down the aisle and safely seated in a pew. "What about Gwenn? She'll be here tomorrow."

"Oh, no, *please!*" It was bad enough to have Gwenn and Bill coming to the wedding, upsetting the whole household by taking Vance's room and crowding Neal and Vance into the sewing room, and moving Rosie down with Ellin.

Gwenn and Bill would quarrel openly and endlessly, of that Susan was sure. And Gwenn would try to run everything. She would step in and reorganize the whole wedding, and when she had caused a complete and utter snafu, she would wash her hands of the whole affair and go wandering about with her gold bracelets clanking and her foot-long cigarette holder spilling ashes over the rug. Susan had made up her mind to bear Gwenn's presence with stoic calm because Gwenn was part of the family, but to look back on her wedding day and always see Gwenn being a big shot in it? No, thank you.

"Oh, no!" she cried, and she added thankfully, "The dress wouldn't fit her anyway. She's a good inch-and-a-half taller than you are, and shaped like a pencil. I would like to use your dress in the wedding, though, Alcie," she explained earnestly, "to keep the yellow-shading-into-bronze theme that you and Jenifer used for your fall weddings. It's becoming almost traditional, like the pink weddings the Parrishes have. If we asked Gwenn to wear it, she'd probably show up in a red, sequined sheath."

"I guess you're right." Alice was happy to supply her dress, so long as she didn't have to be inside it, and she offered the suggestion, "Do you suppose if we call Jenifer in England, she'd change her mind and fly over for just a couple of days?"

"Uh-uh, there isn't a chance," Susan shook her head and said, sighing, "Jen wants to be here just as much as we want her, but Cyril's doing something in Parliament for the next month or two, and to fly all the way over alone, for just a few days, isn't practical. She would so much rather come with Cyril and little Jill at Christmastime, when they can visit around for at least a month. Jen's out. Perhaps, though," she said thoughtfully, "I could ask Tippy. I do love Tippy so much, and I'm marrying her brother. Are you *sure*, Alcie, that you won't feel better by Saturday?"

"Not a chance!" Alice was thankful to have Susan find a satisfactory substitute so nearly her own size, and she said, "My dress may need a little alteration for Tip, but not too much. My waist seems to have gotten larger since I bought it, and it's pretty tight on me. The length's all right, and we've always worn the same size shoes. My matching sandals will fit her, so go call her."

"Shall I? It's final if I do," Susan said, watching Alice nod. And then she smiled with remembering. "I got squeezed into Tippy's wedding at the last minute, and the pattern seems to be repeating itself."

"Just get everything settled before Gwenn shows up and wrecks it," Alice begged. "Do it now, and have the dress fitted. I'll explain the rush to Gwenn if my strength holds out, but contact Tippy. Should she have broken a leg or something since last night, commandeer Penny or Carrol."

Susan hopped up and looked down at poor, peaked little Alice who had always been bouncing with health. Alice was so happy in her miserable state that Susan couldn't feel sorry for her, not really, so she leaned over to drop a loving kiss on tumbled brown bangs, and said, straightening, "Here I go to telephone, so keep your fingers crossed."

Tippy sounded pleased to be asked to take Alice's place as matron of honor, as nearly as Susan could tell from a garbled conversation. Bobby had cut in on the upstairs extension, and his interruptions were no help and bore no relation to the hurried plans they were trying to make. He had been told to stay away from the Jordon menage until time to arrive as a guest, but by luck and good fortune he was unexpectedly in.

"I'll be right over," he kept repeating, while Susan tried to explain how sick poor little Alice was and Tippy was prescribing a remedy her doctor in Panama had given her before Tippy Two was born. "I'll come right over and get the dress and bring it back here," he said, when the conversation had finally reached the necessary change in wedding plans. "Mums can sew it up. Hold everything, I'm coming."

"Bobby, get off the line!" Tippy had lost patience, and she ordered, *"Get off!"*

"But it's half my wedding," he argued, explaining his right to not only listen in but to dip in. "Susan said so. And it's important to me to be sure we've got a matron of honor. You can bet you'd have butted in if I'd got sick for your wedding and we'd had to scrounge around for someone to take my place. This is the only wedding I'll ever have and I'm *interested* in it."

"Oh, all right!" Tippy gave up and shouted above his persistent voice, "I'll love to fill in for Alcie, Susan, and we'll be over right away. I'll have to bring *him* with me. Good-bye."

"Well!" Bobby came loping down the stairway and stood over her as she still sat holding the silent receiver. "This is luck," he said amiably. "Get your tape measure and paper of pins, or whatever you have to take with you, and let's go. They may invite us to spend the rest of the afternoon."

"Not today." Tippy replaced the receiver, looked through the large back window at Peter, swinging his daughter in a rope swing he had hung from the limb of a tree, then got up and swept past Bobby to the side porch. Her mind was on Susan; and when she called to Peter, "I'll be back in a few minutes," she was still thinking of a girl who was doing, and who had always had to do, everything for herself.

"Poor little thing," she said as she rode along with Bobby, looking at him and remarking pointedly, "I hope you take decent care of Susan, she's never had anyone else to."

"I *know* that!" Bobby sounded cross because he felt so tender. "I'm making my whole life over to suit her," he growled; and for him that was quite an admission.

"Yes, you really are." Tippy nodded, then said in sudden surprise, "Why, Bobby, you're doing exactly that. I haven't given you much credit for it."

"Why should you? The Army threw Susan a curve, so she doesn't like it," he said, shrugging. "I haven't been in it long enough to know whether I do or not, so what the heck? Don't go getting any idea that I made The Great Supreme Sacrifice," he admonished, scowling even more fearsomely, lest she switch him from her pet monster to an awkward hero. "I'm not ambitious. I don't want to work up to having eagles or a row of stars on my shoulders. You miss too much of life that way. The kind of life Susan wants suits me: nice home—thanks to the families—kids, an evening out now and then, and eventually owning a business. Dad sure lost the ball when he got David and me, didn't he?"

He grinned cheerfully at her and drove faster toward his beloved. But when he and Tippy ran up the side steps the conference inside had grown. Alice still lay on the sofa with her matron-of-honor dress draped over a chair, but Rosie was folding up the card table and Bitsy was arguing hotly.

"I don't see any reason," she declared righteously, pausing only for a brief hello, "why Bill and Gwenn should come out here two whole days ahead of time. I was glad to give up my room to Jon and Alcie, and to move in with you, Susan, but where am I going to put Anne? You said I could ask her over to stay, and I did."

"Oh, dear, I forgot about her." Susan ran her hands frantically through her hair, saying, "Hi, come in," while she wondered if a cot could be squeezed into her alcove.

All the brides she had ever read about, in novels and short stories, wakened in their beautiful rooms on their wedding morning to someone saying, usually a mother, "I brought your breakfast up, darling, and you're to lie here and rest." Curtains were drawn then, and the bride was left to lie in a luxurious state of languor. Pooh. That was only in fiction. Susan could see herself getting up and falling over a cot while she tried to pack a suitcase. "Oh, gosh, let her come," she said wearily, wishing she and Bobby could elope.

But Rosie unexpectedly spoke up. "It's nice of you folks to come over," she said, just as if she had parted from Tippy only yesterday, clapping a table leg shut and pushing her ridiculous cap back all in one gesture. "We've got more people here than the house will hold, and Ellin and I were saying only this morning that it don't seem right for the General to be so undiscommoded, with his own private bathroom and all, while the others go flyin' around like a flock of birds lookin' for a branch to light on. It seems to Ellin and me that Susan ought to have her room to herself."

"Hasn't she got it?" Bobby asked.

"Not so's you'd notice it," Rosie answered, picking up her table and preparing to depart. "Susan's always the last to get anything around here." And with that piece of information she shrugged, gave Bobby a wink, and hustled out with her table.

"Well, now, just a minute." Bobby took her hint and said forcefully, "Our house is full, but Penny's isn't, and David's isn't. We'll just move the old boy over to one place or the other."

"Oh, not Daddy!" Susan pushed Alice's dress aside and sat down in the chair with it. "I know Rosie means well," she said, looking up, "but she's only upsetting things worse than they are. Daddy's my father. He offered to go to a hotel but I wouldn't let him. He's the one who matters most when I'm getting married. He's—my father."

"I realize that, pet," Tippy put in quickly. "You need him here, just as I needed Mums and Dad around when I was getting married. But, look. Why don't we send Bitsy and her friend somewhere else to relieve the congestion? Carrol has rooms she never uses, and Penny would love to have them. Oh, honey," she said, going over to put a loving arm around Susan and say, "I don't see why someone didn't think of it sooner. We'll ship them over to Carrol's. It's all settled, and now I'll try on the dress."

Susan sighed. She could see Bitsy scowling like a sky about to shoot a clap of thunder because neither she nor Vance would be happy. Davy would be where Anne was and Vance would still be here; Keith, too, if he came to the wedding early. "I don't think that would work," she said, wondering if she dared speak up and publicly tell the reason. "You see . . ."

But Bobby stepped in. "Then send over Gwenn and her movie actor fellow," he suggested. "They're really the ones who're upsetting everything, aren't they?"

"Yes," Susan agreed dully.

"Gladstone is a lot more fitten for Gwenn than Gladstone Gates," he pointed out, not bothering to argue with her. "We'll put Bitsy and Anne somewhere and you can keep your room. Listen, Daffy-dilly." He went over to lean on the already crowded chair and said softly, "You're the only one I care about. Saturday is our big day. I've got my folks, so I want you to have peace and quiet with your dad. If anyone doesn't let you have it, if anyone so much as whispers that the cake hasn't come or complains that the decorations look gosh-awful, or upsets you one little bit on Saturday, he's got me to answer to. Get that?" he asked, glaring at Bitsy. "Susan will be taking pot luck with me after Saturday night, but by gum, until then she's entitled to the best you have to offer."

"You're exactly right, Bobby." Alice found a sudden flow of strength that sat her up to say, "I'd move out but it wouldn't help. It's much better for Gwenn and Bill to go somewhere else, and if somebody will only take them in I'll send them on with my blessing. Shall we consider it settled," she asked, "so Tippy can try on my dress?"

"Yes, and I'm sorry to have caused so much trouble," Bitsy said, pausing for Susan to reply, "Oh, you haven't, darling." But Susan didn't. She simply got up and disappeared into the dining room with Tippy and the dress. And Bobby began talking with Alice. He sat in the chair beside her, and Bitsy thought Alice had suddenly perked up and was feeling much better. People always felt better, or worse, after a talk with Bobby. She, herself, always seemed to feel worse. "I think I'll go outside," she said; and no one noticed her leave.

Vance was cutting across the lawn, headed for the kitchen, so she strolled along until he caught up with her. "Alcie's sick," she said, when they met at the back steps.

"Sure, I know it." He pulled open the screen door and crowded in ahead of her; and before she could inform him of the change in wedding plans he had stopped dead, pointing like a bird dog. "Is that all *trash*?" he demanded, slapping his school books on the counter and staring at a mountain of cardboard boxes and paper, and a full can of garbage. "Do you think I'm going to spend the rest of my afternoon carting that out and burning it?"

"It has to be done, Vancey," Ellin said calmly, "so the sooner ye start the sooner ye'll finish. We're havin' a party tonight, ye know."

"Yeah." Vance stepped around the pile and opened the refrigerator door to look for anything that might restore his failing strength, and Ellin passed him the chocolate tart she had on a plate ready for him.

"Rosie's been burnin' the trash at intirvals all day," she said, "because the widdin' prisints keep comin' in, so 'tis glad we are to see ye. Hop to it, lad."

"Why didn't Queen Elizabeth help?" Vance asked, pointing his tart at Bitsy.

"She was at school, too, Vancey, and thire's been a bit of confirince goin' on inside. What with Gwinn comin' and not enough rooms to go around . . ."

"I won't move again!" Vance shouted.

". . . and little Miss Anne to be here . . ."

"I'll move."

He gave a last swallow, licked chocolate from his lips and bent to shove wadded paper deeper into a box as he said, "Hoist a load there, Bits. Didn't you hear Ellin say that we're giving a party?"

Bitsy sighed and picked up a box, the smallest

one. She couldn't pass on any news to Vance unless she stayed with him, so she followed him outside. "Tippy's going to have to be Susan's matron of honor," she said, while he poked cardboard into the incinerator.

"Yeah? How come?" It didn't matter to him who was in the wedding because he had refused to dress up in the crummy old uniform that Claymore Academy had issued to its students for a sort of junior military training. No uniform and no saber, so no ushering job. He was quite free to sit beside Anne in the bride's side of the church, with Davy safely across the aisle with the groom's family.

"Poor little Alcie," Bitsy said, "she's awfully sick. I'd just die if something should happen to me so I couldn't be in the wedding."

"You're probably dying anyway, because you can't be the bride and show off," Vance retorted, nudging her out of his way while he lighted a match. And he stepped back from the roaring tower of flame he had ignited, not knowing that the angry fire he had started in Bitsy's breast was blazing ten times higher.

CHAPTER 11

BITSY ALWAYS ENJOYED going to parties at Gladstone. It was pleasant to have Perkins' nephew step forward to take the car and drive it away, and to have Perkins himself throw open the great carved doors and say, "Good evening, Miss Bitsy," then open the drawing-room door for her. Guests simply walked in at Gladstone Gates, the hall being in plain view of the living room; and this formal entrance always reminded Bitsy of the parties Jenifer gave in her castle in England.

Tonight Perkins had two carloads of Jordons to greet. He said, "Good evening, General," and was about to add, "I trust you're feeling better, Miss Alice," when Gwenn swept down the stairway, uttering little hostessy exclamations of pleasure.

"Darling!" she cried to her father, who hadn't come home from his office when she and Bill had driven up from New York and, pleased with the change in plans, had grandly ordered their chauffeur to take them straight on to Gladstone. "You're looking wonderful, darling!"

"Just about the same as I did last month when I saw you between planes," the General returned dryly, trying to pass his Homburg around her to Perkins.

"And Alcie, my pet," Gwenn cooed, undaunted. "You're positively blooming!"

"So are you," Alice answered, wishing Gwenn would move on so she could go in and sit down.

Gwenn blocked the way. She trailed cascades of white lace. Her bright yellow hair was upswept into a swirl of bang that was anchored with a diamond comb. Diamond earrings dripped almost to her shoulders and diamond bracelets had replaced the clanking gold ones she wore in the daytime. Her white lace gown had cost five times as much as Susan's wedding dress; and Bitsy, with her first ballerina-length formal crushed in a blue mist against the wall, glowered at her.

"It looks like a wedding dress," she whispered to Susan, who, as the guest of honor, wore the simple sea-green chiffon she had bought for her trip to the Orient and put away to keep for her trousseau. "It has long lace sleeves and a high neck. I think she shows very poor taste."

"Oh, let her enjoy it," Susan whispered back, patiently waiting her turn, which would be after Gwenn had finished showing how important she was. "The poor kid never had a wedding dress."

And she accepted Gwenn's kiss that merely brushed her cheek.

"I'm always so frightfully late," Gwenn apologized, knowing that greeting her family in the hall was far more dramatic than blending in with the wealthy Carrol and the famous Penny in the drawing room, and so having planned it. There were already too many in there. She would have been only one among many: not a movie star like Bill, or an actress, or even a doting mother. Just skinny Gwenn, who had never amounted to much.

"Come, darlings," she said, and motioned regally for Perkins to open the drawing-room doors.

David began to chant, "Here comes the bride," and in the confusion, while Susan was being kissed and Alice hustled to a comfortable spot on a pink brocaded sofa, Bitsy fell back to the end of the line where, as the youngest, she belonged. Then Davy came through a door at the back of the hall. He wore a dinner jacket like the others of his sex, but he was eating a carrot.

"Hi," he said, offering her a bite. "Some doings."

"Oh, isn't Gwenn horrid?" Bitsy cried, shoving away the carrot and shuddering.

She hadn't seen Davy since their afternoon after school, two days before, but she was sure she still knew him. "I wish Gwenn hadn't come to the wedding," she sighed. "She'll wreck it."

"Not with Uncle Bobby around. Take a look." Davy pointed with his stub of carrot as he and Bitsy stopped in the drawing-room door.

Bobby and Susan stood at one end of the long

gracious room, holding court. Family crowded around them, with Lang and Joshu in their dark blue suits and Parri looking like a pink organdy fairy bobbing about. Gwenn couldn't have squeezed in had she tried.

She didn't. She stood regally alone, and, not knowing she was being watched, her face expressed only tired sadness.

"Poor Gwenn," Bitsy said, with a sudden swing to pity. Then she turned back to Davy. "Vance said he isn't going to stay any longer after dinner than he has to," she told him. "He said he'd take us to a party at Twink Matthew's house if we want to go. Do you?"

"No, thanks."

Davy shook his head and for a minute Bitsy felt rebuffed. Perhaps he really was odd and stuffy, she thought. Perhaps she had simply caught him off guard when she had appeared so unexpectedly at the stables. Perhaps he liked being alone to moan and groan over his mismatched legs. Then let him.

She moved on with her head high, her lips ready for smiling greetings to Carrol and David, to her Aunt Marjorie and Uncle Dave, but Davy touched her arm. "I only thought we could have more fun here," he said shyly. "I'd planned to challenge you to table tennis, and Mom had the big family room cleared for dancing. I thought I wouldn't be scared to try it with you, and Mom thought so, too. She was kind of excited about having the rugs taken up and the floor waxed.

They're going to dance at Twink's too, but I told him I couldn't come."

"Oh, Davy, I'd much rather stay here!" Bitsy's relieved laugh sounded like high tinkly notes on a piano. "Why didn't you *say* so?" she stopped to ask. "I was embarrassed."

"For Pete's sake, why?"

Davy had felt so companionable with Bitsy during these last two days, planning to surprise her by coming out of his miserable shell that so distressed his parents. He had even gone so far as to mentally rehearse walking up to her and saying casually, as Vance or any other boy would, "How about a dance, Bits?" Now they had made a production of it.

"I thought I had been forward," Bitsy said, sounding as quaint as Ellin but not caring now, since Davy was still the same Davy who would understand. "I'd practically asked you for a date." And she added confidentially as they started on again, "You know, we'd have had to change back into ordinary daytime clothes if we'd gone with Vance. He said he wouldn't be caught dead outside of here in a dinner jacket. You're much more adult than he is, Davy."

The dinner that would have been extremely formal by Gladstone Gates' standards moved easily along in the delightful Gladstone way. Eighteen sat at the long table in the dining room, and Parri, Lang, and Joshu had been banned behind the closed door of the breakfast room. Crystal sconces along paneled walls lighted the big room beyond the dozens of flickering candles in tall silver candelabra on the dining table, and Perkins kept a watchful eye on his two serving maids.

Courses came on and plates were changed; and David said to Susan on his right, "I'm glad you and Bobby won't be leaving us for very long after Saturday. The guy's really meant for business, just as I was." And he turned to his mother on his left, as he asked, "Do you think Dad's upset because there isn't anyone left to follow in the Army pattern—unless Lang takes a notion to up his grades and get into West Point?"

"Not too much." Marjorie Parrish shook her brown head and smiled the sweet smile she had bequeathed to Penny, the one that made women in Penny's audience go home and practice. "Dad's an intelligent man, David," she said. "He realizes that every time a new generation is born the urge for the Army is lessened by half. My father was a businessman, your father's mother came from a family of farmers. It sounds very complicated, but it isn't, dear. I think," she said, her brown eyes twinkling, "that even the stubborn British are learning that parents can't force their eldest sons into a mold. That's what's so nice about America," she said, giving his hand a loving pat. "We're a nation of individualists."

"But Peter followed the pattern in our family," Susan leaned forward to point out. "And Neal too. And Vance is planning to. Why should our family stay Army if yours doesn't? Our maternal ancestors are as mixed as yours."

"Peter, yes," Mrs. Parrish answered, looking fondly along the table at her very dear son-in-law. "He's happy in the Army. But Neal? I'm not so sure. He has a lawyer's mind, and unless he can be satisfied in the Judge Advocate General's Department he's quite apt to become restless. Vance?"

All three looked at the scowling Vance whose black bow tie had slipped crooked and whose black lock of hair had dropped with his spirits, and all three smiled. "Heaven help the Army," Susan said, "if Vance decides to run it."

She wondered how David felt about Davy, who would have no chance to decide for himself, who could never weigh the advantages and disadvantages of a military career against the life of a civilian. David's gaze was somber as it rested on his son. Then he saw that Carrol had risen, and he watched Davy grin at Bitsy and take her hand while they waited for the elders to precede them.

"The kid'll make it," he said, holding Susan's chair for her while she slid out. "I've been wanting to tell your father and you how grateful I am to Bitsy for what she's done for him."

"Bitsy?" Susan saw Bobby coming for her as fast as his long legs would bring him, but she stared up at David. "Ellin told me that Bitsy was upset because she had been unkind to Davy," she said.

"I don't know about that, but he's going to dance with her tonight. We've had great doings around here and I had to make a trip to town with a list of special records. Carrol," David said, "is beside herself with joy. I haven't seen her so happy since this polio thing struck us. There'll be dancing in the old house tonight."

"Then you'd better give me back my bride," Bobby interrupted, having been separated much too long from Susan. "Do we open the ball?"

"After coffee." David grinned; and knowing his impetuous brother so well, he admonished, "Take it easy, chum. You'll have the rest of your life with Susan."

"It isn't long enough."

Bobby pulled Susan along with him, and as they were crossing the hall she asked, "Aren't I supposed to take your arm, walking gracefully and chit-chatting as we go?"

"Not this time. I have it in mind to kiss you, so we're detouring to the library. I can't kiss you with people passing by."

"Since when?" she asked. "I've never noticed you being shy on planes, trains, ships, street corners, or in hotels, railroad stations or either my house or yours. I've ducked you for years, so when did you get so suddenly shy?"

"Since of this minute, and because I have a lot of things I want to talk over with you. I'm not quite certain in my mind," he explained as she obediently turned into the library with him, "if, when we swing around to leave the church, I'm supposed to get out of the way of your train or if it's your job to get it out of the way of poor nervous me."

"You'll find out exactly what you're to do at the rehearsal tomorrow night," Susan told him soothingly, and she was about to take his dear naughty face between her hands when Parri rose up out of a deep leather chair.

"Well, hi, punk," Bobby said. "What are you doing in here?"

"I'm too ashamed to come out," Parri answered. Her face was streaked with tears and the pink ribbon that bound her unleashed brown hair had slipped down over her bangs. "Joshu upset his milk on my dress."

"Let me see, sweetie." Susan bent down to look at the crushed folds of Parri's full skirt, and said, straightening them out, "Oh, dear, he certainly did, didn't he?"

"He was being silly and showing off," Parri said miserably. "Lang told him to stop but he wouldn't. I look awful!"

"Oh, no you don't." The skirt was indeed streaked with long splashes of milk, but the organdy was nylon, so Susan said, "We'll go in the powder room and I'll have you as good as new in fifteen minutes. Sorry, Robert, old boy." And she led Parri away.

"Mummy's going to murder Joshu," Parri said conversationally, watching Susan lay a towel under the stains and sponge lukewarm water through it. "She told him he couldn't come unless he promised to behave, and now she'll yank him out and murder him."

Susan was sure that Penny would have hurried

off to do exactly what she was doing, which was sponging and drying, sponging and drying; and while she hated to dash Parri's hopes, she said lightly, "Oh, I think she'll let him live. But you were sweet not to run and tell her. It's sure to lighten his punishment if your mother sees that you're not ruined."

"It will?" Parri's eyes clouded for a moment, then she said, "I suppose I shouldn't want him clobbered, although this is my very best dress. It's three inches below my knees, you see, and my wedding dress will be six inches. I'd die if it had been that one. Is the milk coming out?" she asked, bending over to look.

"All out. There you are." Susan shook the skirt to dry it even more than towels had, then let it come carefully to rest on Parri's stiff, lacy petticoats. "My advice is to walk around for a while," she said, "so you won't crush it while it's still a little damp."

"But, Lang has invited me to dance," Parri answered, kissing Susan as she stood up. "I've learned a lot of steps in dancing school and I hope Lang knows what he's doing. Oh, thank you, thank you! I probably would have died without you."

"You wouldn't have gone that far but you might not have been happy." Towels lay in a heap; and looking in a cabinet for more to replace them, Susan said, "Run along and have a good time, honey."

"Thank you—Aunt Susan." Parri opened the door to back out, then paused with her mother's sure flair for a dramatic exit line. "I'm truly thankful that you're going to be my aunt," she said, "instead of one of those creeps Bobby was always bringing to our house."

"Thanks, sweetie." Susan finished her cleaning up and thought she might as well repair her lipstick while she was there. Bobby could wait a little longer for his kiss. But when she walked along the hall again she saw Bitsy and Davy going out the front door. "You aren't leaving us, are you?" she asked.

"Oh, no. It's just so lovely out," Bitsy answered, "that we're going for a stroll in the garden. Jenifer's guests often did after dinner and—well, Davy and I thought we'd do it."

"It's a lovely idea," Susan called, but they didn't hear her.

They went across the terrace and down the wide shallow steps, around the circular driveway that had a fountain bubbling away in the center of it, and across the lawn. Bitsy's blue tulle looked softly luminous in the moonlight, and her curls shone silvery gold.

"You liked living with Jenifer, didn't you?" Davy asked, when they had reached a large garden enclosed by a clipped hedge and were walking along its wide graveled paths.

"Oh, I did." Bitsy smiled with remembering. "I loved the graciousness of it, I suppose." And she turned her head to ask, "Don't you?"

"Don't I what?"

"Like being rich and living at Gladstone?"

"I don't know, I've never thought about it." Davy had always had money, and for almost as long as he could remember he had had the aftereffects of polio. He would gladly live in a cabin in the woods if it could cure his limp, and his parents would gladly give everything they had to have him healthy and sound again.

"I suppose all this will be yours some day," Bitsy said wistfully. "Since you're the oldest son."

"Like inheriting the crown? Uhhuh." Davy grinned, then said, "It depends on which one of us takes over the farming. Dad's a nut on farming, and I'll probably have to be the one. I like it, and Lang can handle Mom's investments and the business end. Say," he suddenly said, teasing, "since you're so nutty about this place, maybe you'd better hold off on any marrying deal and wait for me."

"Thank you, I'll think about it." Bitsy's answer was pert and light, but the suggestion was worth consideration. Davy was a good-looking boy and would be a fine, handsome man. Susan was marrying a Parrish, so why shouldn't she? The *rich* Parrish. "Perhaps we should go back now," she said, suddenly wanting to try out his dancing, and not quite knowing if it was Davy in the moonlight or Davy sitting on a pile of gold that interested her.

"He is sweet," she told herself when they were back inside and walking along a corridor that led to a large paneled room that Carrol always referred to as "the family room" because it was comfortably furnished and made a pleasant gathering place. "If I were older it wouldn't be hard to fall in love with David, so perhaps . . ." She was ashamed as she remembered Keith who had filled her heart and mind only last week. Handsome, unhappy Keith. "I'm fickle," she told herself miserably. "I'm an opportunist. But I'm Bitsy. I lived this way once and I want so much to live this way again."

She stood watching Davy who had gone over to adjust the stereophonic speakers on each side of the record player, and saw Gwenn dancing silently around with her Bill. Gwenn was an opportunist, too, she thought, but Gwenn had missed somewhere. Poor Gwenn. She had leaped too fast. She had snatched Bill because she thought he could help her career and would see that she became famous, too. I wouldn't do that, Bitsy thought, watching how beautifully Gwenn danced. I wouldn't marry Davy just to have Gladstone. I don't think I could.

Davy came back and saw her eyes following Gwenn. "You want to risk my bumping into them?" he asked.

But Bitsy gave him an unexpected reply. "Gwenn really is a beautiful dancer," she said. "Madame Savitskaya, who was the most perfect première danseuse of all the ballets in Europe and here, said that Gwenn not only had perfection of movement but she had the 'spark,' whatever that is. Gwenn studied with her until she got tired of *working* to make the grade and ran off and married Bill. Poor Gwenn. That one sudden impulse to get where she wanted to be through a husband who was a young academy award winner ruined her. She wrecked herself, Davy."

"It often happens," Davy said, watching the once-beautiful Gwenn, too. "We get our sights set wrong and press the button. Plink, no picture. Are you ready for me to take pieces out of your blue satin slippers?"

"Yes, let's dance."

Bitsy pretended enthusiasm but she wondered what Davy was thinking. Had he been astute enough to read her thoughts about making a proper marriage, or was he simply willing to take a stumble around the floor and have it over with? Then she remembered that he was Davy, proud and brave, and that he considered these next few minutes to be a test of what he could do in the future.

"Why, you dance beautifully," she said, surprised when he expertly skirted Gwenn and Bill, who were here, there and everywhere, and even Parri and Lang who had suddenly appeared. And she drew back to scold, "Davy Parrish, you didn't tell me the truth. You said you hadn't ever danced before."

"I haven't. Not even with Mom. Lang helped me some, but he's rock 'n' roll stuff, so I bought some records and practiced. I thought if I do okay I'd ask Mom to dance. She's a swell gal, Bitsy, but she never seems to stop grieving because her little boy can't do what the other boys do."

"She loves you so much."

"I know she does. Dad and I talk about it sometimes. You know, she had a nervous crack-up after the doctors pulled me through, and she's never been really gay and happy since. She worries about me too much, but she's all steamed up tonight, and Dad and I think that if I can start doing things with a gang—wearing shorts, you know, and not caring what I look like—she'll go all out with joy."

"It's hard for you though, isn't it Davy?" Bitsy asked while they stood marking time.

"Yeah. I couldn't make up my mind to do it," he answered, "until you came along. You sort of shamed me into it."

"I'm glad." Bitsy smiled at him and tightened her hand in a squeeze on his shoulder. "Perhaps we can help each other," she said. "If I'm good for you, Davy, you surely must be good for me."

CHAPTER 12

"THERE'S A CLOUD in the sky!" Susan shouted, running pellmell down the stairway Friday afternoon. "It isn't very big but . . ." she swung around the newel post and panted from the living-room archway ". . . it's coming from the west and it's moving fast."

"That's what Jonathan just told me." Alice, in her special spot on the divan, sat up. "Oh, I feel so *useless*," she groaned.

"There's nothing you can do unless you can hold great chunks of the sky back," Susan told her, going to the window and peering upward. "The weatherman on my radio predicted rain this afternoon, with clearing late tonight and probable showers tomorrow."

"He's usually wrong."

"But I can't risk it. We can't have wedding guests plodding around in wet grass and keeping their raincoats on in case the skies should suddenly open up again."

"Then take Plan B." Alice lay down again, but she suggested, "Call Daddy and ask him what to do."

"He couldn't help me decide. And Bobby's gone to the airport to meet his ex-roommate, and to Grand Central to pick up Tony Carstairs. Peter and Tippy went off somewhere to spend the day with some friends of theirs, and Aunt Marjorie's lunching in town with Uncle Dave. Oh, darn it," Susan said, coming back to stand before Alice, "why does the whole family have to go away when I need to call a meeting? I wonder if all the umbrellas and lawn chairs and things have come from Gladstone."

"Ask Jon, he's out on the terrace." Alice sat up again around a wave of nausea, and called, "Jon? Jon?"

"Coming," Jonathan had been giving the side terrace the scrubbing of its life, and he sidestepped a pail of water to put his head inside the screen door and ask anxiously, "Are you all right?"

"She's fine, but we think it's going to rain," Susan answered, going to the door. "We don't know whether to stick to Plan A or take Plan B—the one for inside, you know. And I'm worried about all the things from Gladstone."

"The umbrellas are in the garage and the rest of the stuff is to come on a truck tomorrow morning. Wait till I take off my wet shoes."

Jonathan scuffed around at the door then came

inside, barefooted and with his old khaki trousers rolled up to his knees. "It's getting blacker," he said, "and a big drop just hit me ker-plop. I think you'd better plan for both inside and outside, Susie."

"Oh, dear." Susan sat down and rested her hands on her bare knees below her red shorts.

"It's been so lovely," she said. "Just so beautiful and Septemberish, with good weather predicted for at least another week." Then she looked about her. "This really is an enormous room," she said thankfully, "if we take all the furniture out. But will it hold a hundred people? And where are we going to put the furniture and all the wedding presents so we can use the dining room?"

"We've got that figured out, you know," Jonathan said for comfort. "On paper, at least. Wedding presents stacked in your father's room, furniture—except the piano—carted to the basement. Our room and the boys' room slicked up and ready for guests to leave their stuff in, and Rosie at the door to tell them where to go. That's what we wrote down, isn't it?"

"Oh, I guess so, but . . ." Susan stopped and shrugged helplessly. "What if we go to all this trouble and it doesn't rain?" she asked.

"Better to be safe than sorry." Jonathan took a cigarette from a box on the table and moved away from Alice as he lighted it. "It won't bother you, will it, honey?" he asked. And when she shook her head, he blew out a cloud of smoke and said, "We've got enough strong backs among us. Neal will be here, and Vance, and we can call on Peter and Bobby if we need them. But what about the florist?"

"I'll have to phone him right away," Susan decided. "He knows what to do, but his smilax for the stairway has to come from New York, and he'll have to change all his decorations for the bride's table—making everything on a smaller scale, you know—and put more flowers around the house. I'd better hustle."

She got up and went off to telephone, and Alice looked dolefully up at Jonathan. "Poor child," she said. "She tries so hard and just about everything has gone wrong. First I failed her . . ."

"You couldn't help it, darling."

". . . and now this. Jon?" she asked, "do you really think it's going to keep on raining?"

"It looks like it."

They began to plan the simplest way to make things easier for Susan; and when she came back, she said, "Mr. Pett was wonderful. He'd already called the wholesale florist in New York to be sure he can get whatever he needs on short notice. And he'll send his truck right in for it. I'm sorry for poor Daddy," she said, trying to grin. "I had to decide quickly, so he may find himself with a bill for both inside and outside decorations, but it can't be helped. If I'd had the reception at the country club out here it would have cost twice as much. I know it's all a mess," she said regretfully, "and I suppose it's exactly what I deserve for being so determined to have my last party in my own home, to change clothes for the last time in my own room, and to throw my bouquet from my own stairway. Everybody wanted me to be married on Governors Island, the way you and Peter and Jenifer were, but oh, no! Little Susan had to be sentimental."

"You always have been, honey." Alice sat up again to reach for Susan's hand and say, "This house has been so important to you, finding it and keeping it, so why shouldn't you want to start your new life from it? It's all going to work out beautifully."

"Oh, goodness, I hope so. Do you suppose Vance remembered to go for Neal?" Susan asked, looking down at her watch. "He has our car, and yours is having the brakes relined. Bobby should be back by now, but he isn't. If Vance leaves Neal sitting at West Point I'll never forgive him."

"He won't," Jonathan said, as he went to bring his shoes inside and close the door against rain that was blowing in gusts now. "I heard Bitsy ask him before he left for school if she could go with him, and he said he wouldn't have time to pick her up because he didn't want to keep Neal waiting. They'll be along, but we can start moving the wedding gifts upstairs if you're jumpy. How about packing what we can in cartons, ready to go to your new house?"

"We threw away all the cartons," Susan said disgustedly. "Bobby and I thought we'd take a few at a time in a clothesbasket."

"Then haul out a basket and let's start loading it up."

Susan was grateful for Jonathan, just as she had been grateful for him ever since he had married her sister and they, together, had made her feel that she had a home beside the boarding school she loathed. They carried load after load upstairs while Alice lay on the sofa and audibly bewailed her uselessness. Jonathan stopped to kiss her after each trip, and now and then Susan stopped to show her some very special gift, which they each admired. And while they were still trudging up and down, the side door burst open and Bobby sprinted in with his two groomsmen.

"Hey, Daffy-dilly," he called, when she came running out of the dining room, "here's Tony. He can't tell you any more wild tales about things I've done out at Knox because we're both reformed now. And you remember Stretch Jackson."

"Hello, Tony." Susan held out her hand, first to the young officer who had pretended to be a doctor during the ridiculous episode of Bobby's broken arm, then to the other whom she hadn't seen since his cadet days.

She did indeed remember Stretch. Tall, lanky, and with an inexhaustible appetite, he had come home with Bobby for a weekend. She and Trudy had baked enough pies, cakes, and cookies to stock a church food sale, and she had never stopped running from Friday afternoon until seven o'clock on Sunday evening, when they had left.

"Hey, Susan," Bobby would call over the banister, making her run from wherever she happened to be. "Did you order the corsages for our girls?" he would ask when, breathless, she looked up at him. "Yes," she would answer, "for five o'clock," or for six, or four, or whenever she had been told. "Then hop on your bike and go get 'em." And his door would slam. But not for long.

"Susan?" would come the call again. "Bring us up some boodle. Cake and milk will do—and Stretch wants coffee." "Susan? I've got a button loose on my blouse." "Susan?"

It had been "Susan," "Susan," "Susan," from early morning until evening, when they went off to a party, and Susan had thought of changing her name. Mrs. Parrish and Trudy had tried to relieve her, but the call for Susan never stopped.

"Oh, yes, it's nice to see you again," she said now, taking a bony hand and looking at a young officer who hadn't gained enough ounces to fill out his civilian clothes. Then just for the fun of it she said, "Bobby, hop out and ask Rosie to bring in the tea tray. Then you can carry this last clothesbasket of presents upstairs. We're shifting the wedding reception," she went on without waiting to see if he meekly obeyed. "And I want both of you to know my sister Alcie and her husband, Jonathan Drayton. Alcie, here are Stretch Jackson and Tony Carstairs. You've heard me talk of Tony. He was Bobby's best friend out at Knox."

"But don't hold it against me." Tony smiled engagingly under a dapper black mustache, and seeing Bobby dragging a clothesbasket filled with crystal glasses and goblets thought it wise to hustle over and take one end.

Bitsy and Anne blew in the front door shaking raindrops out of their hair; Vance arrived with Neal; and by the time General Jordon had left his car in the driveway and sidestepped Jonathan's pail on the terrace, Bobby had everything well organized.

"Okay, men, we can take off for my bachelor dinner now," he said, "the General's here. Hi, General."

Bobby had been determined to do this wedding in the style Emily Post had set down as correct. The groom should give a bachelor dinner, she had written, or at least custom had decreed it, so he would give one. The only drawback had been that he had very little time to spend on planning it, and no money. So he had looked around the family for a substitute host, and David had been his victim.

"I'll get 'em all over to Gladstone early," he had said a few days before, sitting in the car and discussing it with Susan, "and then I can hustle 'em on to the church for the rehearsal. Do you really think I have to give my ushers souvenirs of this great occasion when they ought to be glad to take part in it for nothing?"

She had said he did, since that was also custom, and he had reluctantly agreed. "But nothing expensive like the imported evening bags you're giving your gals," he had declared. "I saw some darn good-looking cuff links for five dollars a pair, and that's what they get. All but two of them are family, so why should I put out a lot of dough?"

So David was giving the bachelor dinner, and Bobby was determined that it should begin on schedule and end in a hurry. General Jordon and Jonathan were grudgingly given time to change their clothes; Bobby assured Neal that he would be quite comfortable in his cadet uniform and told Vance that he looked fine in his school blazer, so to hurry up and back his car out of the way.

"See you at the church, Daffy-dilly," he called to Susan as he rushed his reluctant group out. Then with them safely on the outside, he ran back to kiss her. "Man, oh, man, but I'm busy," he said importantly. "Now don't you gals hang around at Penny's and be late."

"We won't," she promised. "Penny's having a quick buffet, and the church is only up the road a little way from there. We'll be there at nine."

"Well, see that you are. I'll have my group there at a quarter of."

He kissed her hurriedly again; and watching him leap the terrace steps she wasted a precious minute to think how strange it was that about this same time tomorrow evening she would be going wherever he went, forever and ever, and it would be her own family she would have left.

"I wish you were going to Penny's with us," she said, turning back to Alice, who was alone now. "Are you sure you won't be lonesome? It seems so heartless to leave you here by yourself."

"Ellin's here," Alice answered, "and I've been wanting to have a good talk with her, and, oh, I almost forgot to tell you. Gwenn telephoned and said she'd rather have a tray here with me than go to Penny's. She said she wanted to talk."

"Well, mercy on us." Susan immediately thought that the unpredictable Gwenn was hurt because she hadn't been asked to be in the wedding, but even as she began, "Was she . . ." Alice shook her head.

"It's been so long since Gwenn and I have really talked," she said wistfully. "Not since we were little girls, it seems. Since long before she ran off and got married. And I thought she was different last night, later in the evening, I mean. She didn't fuss with her make-up, and she was awfully quiet and kept watching all of us as if her mind was a million miles away. She looked like the Gwenn I used to love so much. And when we were leaving, she whispered, 'I've missed you so, Alcie. Let's be close again. I'll find the time.' "

"I'm glad she did, darling." Susan bent over the sofa and laid her cheek on Alice's brown hair. "It's worth your missing the evening," she said, "if you can bring Gwenn back to us. Perhaps after I'm married," she added, reminded of the passing of time and straightening up, "I won't seem so young to her, and can help. Tell her I love her. And now I've got to run up and dress."

The time at Penny's flew by. Rain or no rain for tomorrow was the paramount topic of conversation, and the town hall's old clock in the village was just bonging out nine hoarse strokes when Carrol pulled her loaded station wagon up beside the church, behind four cars already parked there.

"Here comes that crazy son of yours, Aunt Marjorie," Susan whispered to Mrs. Parrish as they shed their raincoats in the vestibule of the quaint little church. "I do hope I can either learn to live with his impatience or slow him down." And she said, "Now Robert Blaine, take it easy. The longer this fun lasts the less time we'll have to lie awake and wait for tomorrow to come."

"But Dr. Wilson has an appointment," he protested, pulling her along the aisle like a caveman dragging his mate. "He wants a quick run-through and . . ."

"No wedding ever had a quick run-through," she interrupted, feeling a little lightheaded from all the excitement, but managing to stop them both beside a chubby little man who looked perfectly willing to spend his entire evening talking with Colonel Parrish and her father. "Good evening, Dr. Wilson," she said.

"Oh, good evening, my dear. Robert here tells me that you're all in a great hurry," the minister answered, taking her hand and patting it. "I do hope I haven't delayed you. I was a little late, due to an appointment, but we can begin right away."

"We have until tomorrow afternoon at five o'clock," Susan answered. And she leaned forward to whisper loudly to him, "Bobby's nervous, that's all. He's never been married before and he's in a panic."

"I sure am." Bobby was willing to admit his nervousness, but he garnished it with, "I think the whole business is a barbaric custom. All this pomp and fuss and foolishness, with people who didn't want to come in the first place just sitting there and staring at you like you're something pitiful. There ought to be an easier way to get married."

"There is, my boy." Dr. Wilson smiled and said,

"If you and Susan would like to slip in here tomorrow morning, I can tie the knot in five minutes."

"Not on your life." Bobby knew he was caught, so he grinned. "I want the works, Reverend," he said, "but there's just one change I'd really like to have made. Can you do it?"

Dr. Wilson had turned away to David who had said something to him, so he asked the question of Susan instead. "Could we leave out just one little sentence in the ceremony?" he asked uncomfortably. "I'll come out strong with 'I do,' and the I-promise-to-love-and-cherish part, but, gosh, I've been to a lot of weddings and I always break out in guffaws at one certain question the groom gets."

"What one's that?" Susan asked, watching him fidget.

"It's the 'With all my worldly goods I thee endow,' " he answered. "I haven't got any worldly goods. Most *young* guys don't."

"You have a half-interest in a house," she reminded, trying not to smile at his seriousness, "and a business plastered with mortgage, and six hundred dollars."

"Five hundred and ninety-five dollars," he corrected. "We discovered at dinner that we've only got five ushers in uniform to make an arch of sabers, and we need six. So Neal called up a cadet who's coming to the wedding, anyway, and to spend the rest of the weekend with him, and he'll do it. I have to buy him cuff links."

"Only five? My goodness, how could we have

miscounted?" Susan looked at different groups and tried to sort out the groomsmen. David, as Bobby's best man, Peter, Neal, and Bobby's two old friends. "Why, you're right!" she cried, not having doubted it.

"Of course, I'm right. We got to practicing the arch deal on our own before dinner and, wow, we didn't have enough to make it. Vance and Davy weren't eligible, so there we were. Now it'll cost me five bucks."

"We'll skip a meal on our trip," Susan said soothingly, "or you can. I'll eat and you can watch me."

She saw David and Peter coming toward them, and gave Bobby a kindly pat as Peter said, "We came for a wedding rehearsal, you know. If you two will stop mooning at each other, we'll get on with it. Aunt Marjorie says she'll play the organ for us."

"Oh, Lord, must she?" Bobby's nerves had come unfrazzled again. To have his mother sitting up there pumping out notes while he stood miserably below her and waited interminable minutes for Susan to come along and hold him up was too much. "Aw, now Mums," he protested loudly, leaping up some steps beside an altar where he wasn't supposed to go until he and Susan made their way up there together, and punching her in the back. "Do you know how to play that thing?" he asked.

"Oh, I think so," she answered, tentatively hitting a note that made the organ blast out a groan. "I haven't done it in years, but I can practice a little. I can play *The Sunshine of Your Smile* and *Down by the Old Mill Stream,* and then leap into *O, Promise Me.*"

She gave him a teasing look that he mistook for confidence, and which made him say, "Oh, gosh, don't hog the show. Beat out the wedding march and quit while you're ahead."

"I'll try, dear. It's so wonderful to play for my son's rehearsal." She pulled out a stop and timidly touched a key. Both stop and key were wrong, and the organ gave a plaintive peep. "Go on, dear," she said, "you make me nervous."

So Bobby went back down and let David lead him in a forceful fashion, just as he had once led Peter, into a small lonely room where he couldn't see what was going on.

The flower girl, the bridesmaid, the matron of honor, and the bride and her father had disappeared into the back of the church. Even peeking out, Bobby couldn't see where they had gone. Penny, pretending to be her mother and the last who would be seated, had walked in on Peter's arm. The organ yodeled *O, Promise Me,* and the ushers marched like soldiers down the aisle. Stretch and Tony came first, then Peter, who would have David on the return trip, and Neal, minus his matching cadet. Bobby, watching them juggle into position in a lopsided semi-circle, was relieved to see Josh get up and sort them out.

"David will stand in here," Josh said to Peter, as if directing a play, "so leave some room for him. Stretch, you and Tony will have to separate, one going left and one right, then the two cadets can each take an end of the line. And remember to leave plenty of room for Bitsy and Tippy and Parri. Let's try again."

The organ gallantly returned to approximately where it had left off, and David jerked Bobby back into his lonely room. "Josh is going to straighten everything out," he said, "and your cue's coming up. Stand still."

"But I'd like to see what Susan's doing," Bobby complained, opening the door an inch. "I won't get to see tomorrow, so I'd like to watch her tonight."

"Okay, go ahead, but don't criticize Mums and make her nervous."

Susan was standing in a puddle of water left by the dripping raincoats and watching the military force unsnarl itself. Listening to her Aunt Marjorie torture the organ was such an experience that she didn't recognize the sudden switch to the Lohengrin Wedding March. Only Mrs. Parrish's nodding head and her lips saying "tum-tum-te-tum, tum-tum-te-tum," brought her to and made her give Parri a starting shove. "Go on," she said, watching Bitsy get ready to start.

Parri was halfway down the aisle, with Bitsy and Tippy following at well-spaced distances, and Susan and her father just entering the church, when Penny jumped up from her pew and ran back to stop her child.

"Don't look around and grin like a Cheshire cat!" Penny cried, holding Parri by her shoulder. "You're not Miss America greeting your public. Keep your eyes straight front and watch where you're going. Now pay attention and do it right."

The organist was unable to start where she had left off this time, so after a few false tries the whole procession went back and started again.

"Don't be nervous, my dear," General Jordon said to Susan, whose hand rested lightly but firmly on his arm. "This is my third trip—hur-rumph—to the altar with daughters, and it's really quite—er—hur-rumph—simple, you see."

"Uhhuh." The procession had been stopped again, this time because Bitsy didn't know whether she should turn left or right.

"Left," Josh shouted, still directing, and she bumped into Stretch and stopped beside him. Tippy pulled up next to her, then Parri found her place; and looking around, Josh asked, "What became of the groom?"

"He's glued to the door," David answered, laughing so hard that he could hardly explain. "He got so busy watching that I just left him there to see what he'd do. I'll hustle him out on cue tomorrow. Hup, Bobby boy."

So the procession went back and tried it once more.

Everything went more smoothly this time, with even the organ keeping less erratic time and the group before the minister falling into place and leaving enough room for the bride and groom to stand. Dr. Wilson was patient in his coaching of Susan and Bobby, and when he said, "I will ask you, Robert, if you take this woman et cetera," Bobby's "I do," bounced against the walls of the church. If he clung to Susan instead of her clinging to him when they mounted the chancel steps to kneel on a pair of white satin pillows that weren't there yet, no one but Susan knew it.

"We're married!" he cried exultantly, after the minister had said, "Now you may kiss your bride," and he had done a thorough job of it.

"Oh, we are not." Susan had to push him forcefully under the imaginary arch of sabers, and when she had him out in the wet vestibule, she shouted above the organ's vociferous bellowing, "Dr. Wilson didn't say, 'I now pronounce you husband and wife.' That's what makes us married."

"Well, I am if you aren't," Bobby contested stubbornly. "I went through a lot to get this far, and God was looking on just as much tonight as He will be tomorrow. I don't see why it wasn't legal."

"Because I didn't wear my pearls," Susan said, knowing that would stop him. "And we gave our beautiful rings back to David."

"Yeah, we've got to have our rings. Okay." Bobby squared his shoulders for another try at this marriage business tomorrow, but he did hold Susan close and whisper, "We are married, dear Daffy-dilly, and we're going to stay married 'until death us do part.' "

CHAPTER 13

SUSAN'S WEDDING MORNING dawned with Susan sitting up in bed and looking anxiously through a closed casement window. It had rained intermittently during the night, as she had been up and down, closing and opening the windows. Now, watching a murky sky that showed the faintest hint of pink in the east where the sun should be rising in full glory, she lay tiredly back on her pillows and decided that the day would be whatever it would be, so she might as well catch a little more sleep. "Good morning, dear room," she murmured as she had never failed to do since this lovely rose-papered bower had become hers, then burrowed down under her blanket.

Pounding wakened her again. Voices, pounding, a truck pulling into the driveway, and a clatter on the lawn. "Oh, mercy me," she said, rolling over to look at her bedside clock. "It's after eight! Good heavens!"

She was sitting on the side of the bed, sleep-dazed and fumbling her feet into slippers, when she heard a light tap and Bitsy opened the door. Bitsy held the wobbly bed tray that was only used when a Jordon was too ill to come to the table, and she said, "Good morning, dear Susan. Happy wedding day. I brought you your breakfast."

"Oh, Bits, how sweet of you!" Susan didn't want the breakfast, but the sight of the tray with its best china coffeepot, a crystal vase with a pink rosebud in it, and Bitsy smiling above it, starchy and fresh in pink cotton, brought a grateful, "You've made me feel like a bride—you know, pampered and special. Thank you, darling."

"You're always so good to everyone else," Bitsy answered, feeling embarrassed but proud too, to have thought of something that would please Susan as much as this seemed to do. "Run brush your teeth while I plump up your pillows, then we can talk. Everything's moving along downstairs so we have plenty of time. It's going to be a beautiful reception, Susan."

"I hope so." Susan took one more glance at the fractious sky outside, then hustled down the hall, belting her robe as she went. "Do you think it's going to clear?" she asked when she came back, her thoughts still on the weather. "It does look brighter, don't you think?"

"Yes, I'm sure it does." Bitsy settled the tray across Susan's knees and sat down on the other bed beside two open, packed cases. "Carrol telephoned early, and we decided," she said importantly, "to scatter the lawn chairs about, and even a few tables for the people who might want to take their supper plates outdoors. She sent us her white, wrought-iron love seats and chairs, too, the lacy ones that look like valentines."

Bitsy had watched the furniture settled in place, had even made sure that a settee was placed far away under a tree. In her mind she could see Keith sitting there, glum and wretched until she could drift out to him and make him know with sweet sympathy how well off he was. "The florist is here, too," she related, realizing that Susan was interested in knowing about the mechanics of the morning, not her own deft handling of Keith. "He has a truckload of palms to go to the church, and his white carpet for the aisle, and dozens and dozens of white candles. The caterer telephoned, and he and his men will be here at two. Everything's set, Susan, so you don't have to hurry."

"Oh, thank you, honey," Susan said again, relaxing enough to pour the fragrant coffee. "Has Bobby called me yet?" she asked.

"He came by and left a letter. It's under your napkin," Bitsy said, pointing. "I thought it ruined the looks of the tray so I laid it under there."

"Oh, good."

Susan forgot her coffee and tore open the sealed envelope to read, *Sorry Bride, but I've got to dash to N.Y. for those darned cuff links and to pick up some old lady friends of Mum's who are too stupid to get here on their own. Thought you should stay in bed as long as you can and told Bitsy so, but ought to be back by noon and will see you. All my deepest love—and it's a darn sight deeper than the ocean. Bobby.*

"Bless his heart," Susan said dreamily, knowing that although the idea of breakfast served in bed might have been Bitsy's, Bobby had started her thinking of it. And to Bitsy's dismay, she took three quick swallows of coffee, put down her cup, and asked, "Where's Ellin?"

"Helping Rosie spread Mother's Venetian lace cloth on the dining-room table," Bitsy replied. "It looks beautiful. And when white gardenias are laid around the cake and the silver candlesticks, it will be quite perfect."

"I have to talk with Ellin," Susan said, setting the tray to one side and hopping out of bed. "This may be my last chance to be alone with her, so suppose you send Rosie up to do my room and I'll dress in a flash and take my coffee down to the kitchen."

"Wouldn't you rather have Ellin come up here?" Bitsy asked, thinking what a waste of effort it had been to set up the tray and carry it so far.

But Susan shook her head. "No," she said, "the fact that you did this for me is what counts. I can go like a race horse all day because of your loving thought." And she added from inside her closet where she was jerking out an old candy-striped dress, "I may be sentimental, and goodness knows I am, but Ellin and I have had some of our closest times sitting together at the kitchen table. I want one last sit, so *please* see that Rosie doesn't knock my wedding dress off its hanger. Run get her, and threaten her with pain of death if she does."

Bitsy ran, and Susan scrambled into her clothes, slapped on lipstick, then gave her curls a quick brush, ignoring the box of rollers and pins that was ready on her dressing table. All that could come later, the fussing over a hot scented bath, the careful setting of hair that wouldn't show under a veil, anyway.

She took a quick turn around the corner of the hall by the stairway, and said, "Oh dear, I'm sorry," as she stumbled over a man who was sitting on the top step twining smilax up the iron posts of the banister. "I didn't step on your hand, did I?" she asked anxiously.

"You missed it by a foot." The man grinned up at her to see if she had caught his joke but she was plunging on down, and saying over her shoulder, "Thanks for doing such a lovely job. It's beautiful!

"Ellin?" she called, racing through the empty living room without seeing the row of palms before which, as Mrs. Robert Parrish, she would stand to receive her father's guests, and past the dining-room table that looked beautiful with its scratches and scars hidden beneath linen and lace, "Oh, Ellin," she cried, pushing open the swinging door to the kitchen and letting herself be stopped by two loving arms that held her against Ellin's ample bosom.

"There now, lovey," Ellin crooned, "don't ye

worry. Iverything is movin' along, and the good Lord is after sindin' us sunshine."

"I'm not worrying about the weather," Susan said. "Nothing can spoil my being married to Bobby, not if it rains or hails. But right now I want to be with you. I want to sit and drink coffee with you, and have you tell me that I'll never be very far away from you."

"That ye shall do."

Ellin moved briskly away and busied herself as she always had when little Jordons had brought her their sorrows and tears, or their gladness and tales of prowess; and when she saw Susan in her special chair at the table, she set a steaming cup of coffee before her and rested a loving hand on her hair.

"Lovey," she said, "my very special lovey of them all, we'll have miny mornin's here whin yere young husband has gone off to his daily business, just as we've always had. We'll be bakin' an' talkin' an' ristin' ourselves."

"I never could go far away from you, Ellin," Susan said, looking up, her blue eyes soft with love. "It would be like—like leaving my mother. You've been that, you know."

"Sure an' I'm glad to hear ye say it. Ye, of all my childrin, have filt it the most, unliss pirhaps it was our Jinifer. Susan and Jinifir," Ellin said, sitting down at her own place and taking off her gold spectacles to wipe a mist from them, "have been most truly me own. Jinifir with her young and overburdened need, thin you. Ah, tis a fine time we'll be havin'," she said lightly, "two weeks from now. Ye'll be Mrs. Parrish when ye come back, will established and important, and we'll sit drinkin' our coffee or tea while we go right on straightenin' out the dear ornery Vance and the insecure little Bitsy. 'Tis goin' to be a beautiful life fir us, lovey."

"It's what I've always wanted," Susan answered soberly, taking a long time to drip cream into her coffee to cool both it and her turbulent emotions. "Bobby gave it to me, bless his precious heart, and I want to keep it as lovely as it is today."

"Ye will. And now pirhaps," Ellin said, knowing when sentiment should be nipped like a beautiful bud from its mother bush, "we had bitter git down to business. We have our immediate plans to consider, now. Whin we go to the church an' come home again . . ."

"You stay in your blue silk dress," Susan ordered. "You sit beside Alcie while I'm being married to Bobby and then you come home and forget to worry. No staying lost in the kitchen. Is that clear?"

"Pirfictly." Ellin knew she would do as she pleased. No one would notice if she disappeared to order the hired waiters about or prod the dazed Rosie into action. " 'Twill all go will," she said complacently, "and I shall feel viry important."

"Well, see that you do." Susan could drink her coffee now, but she pushed away the piece of toast Ellin had made. "I do think it's clearing," she said, jumping up and running to the window.

"It is! Why, there's a definite patch of sunshine. Oh, joy!"

The day flew by. Bobby came in and was hurried out before Susan had a chance to see him. Alice felt so suddenly better that everyone vainly begged her to take her dress back from Tippy; and the sun shone on the grass hotter than an electric dryer in a beauty shop. Plush took an exploratory leap onto the bride's table and was put in the basement, along with Cassius who had found a bone and brought it into the pleasant wasteland of the living room. The florist left and the caterer came with his staff, and Alice suddenly said, "Oooooh, here I go again," and hurried off to lie down. And the telephone rang constantly.

"Keith called," Bitsy dutifully reported to Susan, catching her as she was flying up the stairs to dress. "He asked if there was anything he could do for you."

Keith hadn't asked for Susan directly or intimated that he was suffering in any way. He had simply said that he and his parents were on their way to the wedding and were having a very late lunch in the village, and he had suddenly wondered if there was any last-minute errand he could run to help out. He hadn't sounded as if he was going to sit properly on his bench in the garden either, waiting until the receiving line broke up, because he had merely said, "If this shindig ends early enough, I'll send the folks home with my sister and her husband, and perhaps we can get a crowd together and go on to celebrate somewhere. Is it a date, Bits?"

"Yes—I suppose so," she had answered, hesitating and wondering if Anne and Vance and Davy were to be included, or if it would be just the older crowd that Susan had gone to school with, and Neal's friends. "I'll try to get away," she said, telling herself that Keith was simply being very brave. "We'll plan something, and talk, just as soon as I can slip outside."

But now she stood looking up at Susan who smiled down from above a shower of green, just as she would be doing in five or six hours when she tossed down her wedding bouquet.

"Tell him, thanks, but no, hon," Susan returned, exactly as if Keith might still be on the telephone, and not caring if he was waiting to hear her voice for the last time. "You'd better start dressing now. And, please, try to get Anne out of the bathroom. No, I'll hustle Daddy, then use his." She hurried on, and Bitsy, left looking up at the spot where she had been, closed her eyes and thought. How selfish and inhuman. I never could do it. I never could hurt Keith, or Davy, or anyone the way she has.

And suddenly, after a long day of preparation and rushing about, it was four-thirty. Anne stood pecking out the wedding march on the piano, wearing her new afternoon dress of stiff, rose satin, and Vance, not worrying about black hairs on a black dinner jacket, was trying to catch Plush who had escaped.

"Wow, aren't you something!" he exclaimed, as Neal came in from the kitchen, looking exactly as he did every weekday afternoon when he wore his dress uniform with its tails and brass buttons, and marched in the five-o'clock parade. "Grab Plush as he goes by, if you aren't afraid you'll soil your white gloves. Hey, Jon! Stop him!"

Jonathan, in dinner jacket, too, made a grab for the cat which had leaped past him into the hall and was climbing a green hedge that was the stairway. Plush and smilax came down together; and clutching him, Jonathan shouted, "Alcie! Come quick!"

Doors upstairs opened, and Alice, forgetting how dizzy she was, dashed down, trying to zip up her beige lace dress that had become too tight. "What happened?" she asked. And seeing the near wreckage, she called upward, "Go on back, Daddy, everything's all right. Tell Susan that some smilax fell off, that's all, and we're fixing it."

Plush was finally caught. He meowed and hissed and spat, while howls from Cassius, still jailed in the basement, accompanied him like a wailing saxophone. Vance carried him out and pitched him down some stairs and slammed a door; Jonathan got the zipper on Alice's dress all the way to the top while she held her breath, and Anne flew to work on the stairway. Another door opened above, and Bitsy came down, trailing golden net behind her.

"Susan doesn't want anyone to help her but Ellin," Bitsy said, holding her crown of golden flowers so high and still that she couldn't see the trailing vines on the steps. "She's almost ready. Well, really, Anne, I should think you might move out of my way."

The green vines were put back together. Susan, upstairs dressing, could hear the giggles and grunts, but didn't have time to wonder about what was going on below her. There was so much *dress*. Even when she ducked and Ellin got it over her head, so much lace and net and satin billowed out that she had to fight her way through it.

"Isn't this silly?" she said with a nervous giggle, stepping back onto the white sheet from which she had staggered while she and Ellin were clawing and pulling at four layers of frothy underlinings. "I'll bet Bobby hopped right into his darned blue uniform that he wore to the President's ball."

"Ye look just beautiful," Ellin answered, not seeing that Susan's hair was still in pin curls and that she hadn't put on her lipstick yet.

"With all this train hanging out behind me? Don't be silly. I feel like a manikin in a store window."

"But ye'll have to hurry."

"I know it, darn it." The curls came down, were quickly brushed into place, and the veil which was attached to its coronet of pearls and tiny curled ostrich feathers was settled over them. The coronet was Susan's something old, because it had been Tippy's. Her something blue was the tiny turquoise pin that had been her mother's and it was fastened to the lacy bodice of her slip. "Oh, heavens," she said, having finished with the lipstick. "My pearls! 'The bride wore pearls, the gift of the groom,'" she quoted laughing, trying to see through the fog of net and find the lustrous beads that should be right where her hand could touch them but weren't. "Where *are* the darn things?"

"Ye have thim on," Ellin reminded quietly. "Ye put thim on before the dress, if ye'll remimber. Now stand still so I can straighten out yere train. Stand *still,* lovey."

"I'm too nervous, and I'll muss all up again anyway." Susan thought she looked good enough, as nearly as she could see her reflection through so much fluff, and she asked, "Where's Daddy? I think I'm supposed to have fond last words with him or something." And she tottered off her sheet again.

"Daddy," she called, opening her door to find her father standing hesitantly before it. And she cried, "Oh, Daddy, you look so *handsome!* I wish I could have been old enough to appreciate it when you and Mother went to parties and you wore your special evening dress blues. Oh, Daddy, I wish we could be little again and have Mother with us!"

"I do too, darling," he answered, thinking that she was the most beautiful of his three bride-daughters, and looked almost exactly like her mother had twenty-three years ago. "I—er . . ." He cleared his throat and said, "When I walk down the aisle with you, I shall feel as if Elizabeth is walking beside me."

"Thank you, Daddy." Susan flung back her

veil to kiss him, and said soberly, "We don't have to say good-bye, because I'm coming back to be near you, just as I've always been. Marrying Bobby just means loving one more, that's all. We'd better go now. Oh, Daddy, I'm so proud of you and I do love you so much."

She would have thrown herself against him, veil and all, but he gently held her away. "Those are the things I'm supposed to say to you, daughter," he told her with no hesitancy in his speech, only a deep sincerity. "They are what I say to myself every day. Where would I ever find another child like my loving little Susan? And when I put your hand into Bobby's today," he said, a twinkle coming into his eyes, "I may just add all on my own, 'Here she is, my boy, and if you don't appreciate what I'm giving you I'll thrash you within an inch of your life.'"

"Oh, Daddy." Susan began to laugh softly as he hoped she would. "Every time Bobby does the least little thing I don't like," she said, "I'll rush back home and tell you to thrash him. And I'll tell his father to, too. And his mother can spank him. And Trudy can give him a piece of her mind, and Ellin. I'll be truly spoiled now." And she turned to call, as if reminded that time was passing, "Ellin? You're to ride with Alcie and Jon, you know. We're leaving now. Come on, Daddy, let's not be late for our wedding."

"Well, it's about time!" Neal grumbled, when they came down, arm in arm and rehearsing the way they would walk up the aisle. He had had his special few minutes with Susan, twin to twin, she in an old bathrobe and he in dirt-stained shorts. Each had admitted that the second fork of separation in their path of twinship had been reached and that nothing would ever be quite the same again. Neal had branched off first when he had gone into a man's world at West Point, and now she was going into a very special world of her own, with Bobby.

"We'll always be close though, won't we?" she had asked anxiously, sitting on her dressing-table bench and looking up at him with a clean, scrubbed, little-girl face.

"Why, sure," he had promised, never having doubted it. "I like Bobby, you know that."

"And you'll marry somebody I can like?"

"I'll bring her around and let you inspect her before I ask her," he had said lightly, bending to kiss her. "Just you be happy, twin, and I'll be happy with you. Right?"

"Right—I suppose."

That had been one of the many times today when Susan had wished she were a child again, happy in the moment of tightening her new skates with a new key, swinging a baseball bat with her hands where Neal had placed them, going to a party in her best dress and carrying both Neal's tissue-wrapped present and her own because he was too proud to do it, trying to ask a question above the din of Gwenn's record player, eating chunks of Ellin's cake without ever having heard of calories. There were so many times that she wished she could relive, so many sights and smells and hidden excitements she wanted to recapture. And yet, she knew, ten years from now she would want to remember each minute of this day, each minute of her life with Bobby even though some were sure to hold tears and suffering, just as those happy childhood days had.

"Bitsy, don't forget to stand up in the back of the station wagon," she said, smiling into Anne's worshipful stare. "Vance and Anne will drive you, and Daddy and Neal and I are going in the limousine that Gwenn insisted on sending for us. We'll have to stand up and bend over the front seats."

"Well, let's get the show on the road." Vance, never a patient one to wait, was tired of having Anne pick cat hairs off his jacket when they didn't really show much, so he helped Alice down from the wide window seat where she had been quietly sitting, and said to her, "You'd better put Susan in the car and spread her stuff out, and Anne can fix Bitsy. Let's get going."

There was sudden and noisy commotion. Susan's long train and veil were carefully scooped up and folded over her arm; and before she went out the door Neal held open for her, Susan closed her eyes silently to say, "Good-bye, my own dear house. Susan Jordon is leaving you for a little while, but Susan Jordon Parrish will come back."

CHAPTER 14

THE WEDDING WAS OVER. Susan and Bobby had clung tightly to each other from the moment they had swept gaily back along the aisle, side by side. Even in the limousine with all Susan's train and veil piled on her lap like whipped cream, Bobby had held her hand in both of his and whispered, "Look at our bright new rings, all married to each other. *Look!*"

Susan had looked, but not at the rings. Her blue eyes had lifted to Bobby's face and she had breathed with wonder, "Why, it's part mine. Your face belongs to me. That's funny, isn't it?"

But now, back in the big living room at Gladstone Gates, they were separated. Her hand with its shiny gold ring was holding her bouquet and his was pulling a palm leaf away from the back of his neck while the photographer pointed his camera at the receiving line, and said,

"Now, if you'll all stand a little closer together—that's fine. Please turn around, Major Parrish."

"Who—me?" Bobby was pleased with such rapid promotion, and he leaned out to call down the line to his classmate, "You'd better resign, boy. Look at the rank it gives you."

He was enjoying this. He had gone through a trying experience to get Susan, almost as grim as being shot at in war, but now he was relaxed and having fun. He had her right here beside him, and never again, so long as he lived, would he have to stand in plain sight of a hundred and twenty-three spectators, waiting like a dummy while Susan did that step-hold-step business with Parri poking along in the lead. But it was all right now. Everything had been fine from the moment General Jordon had put Susan's steady little hand in his. Susan had ended his embarrassed misery by smiling confidently at him.

"We're married," he whispered thankfully to her for the eleventh time since they had walked under the arch of flashing sabers. And the photographer told him to look straight ahead and smile.

Pictures were snapped of the whole long receiving line, of the bride and groom flanked only by their parents, of the bride and groom alone. Cars began to arrive, and guests could be seen sauntering about in the late sunshine on the lawn long before the avid photographer was satisfied that he had enough pictures. "Thank you," he said at last; and everyone hopped back into place.

Sometimes Bobby got so interested in playing his new role of husband that he forgot to send people on to his parents beyond him, and he never did bother with names. Those whom he knew he chatted with lengthily, strangers he passed on with a mumbled garble, but he did wholeheartedly agree with anyone who gave him so much as a chance that he was "one lucky guy." He and Keith pumped hands. They grinned and pumped, with Bobby suggesting a get-together as soon as the new house was finished. And Susan smiled frankly and happily at all his old girls. But suddenly it was over.

"Do we borrow Stretch's saber now and cut the cake?" he asked in a whisper, when the long line had broken up and he and Susan were left standing alone before the potted palms.

"After the punch has been passed around," she whispered back, looking something like Susan, but not quite, because her lips were still spread in a fixed smile that might never shrink back into shape. And then to his dismay, she darted off without him.

"Hey, Daffy-dill . . ." he began; then his smile, too, grew wider. "She can't get away," he said to Bitsy's funny little boss in the bookshop who had fluttered over like an injured bird to tell him how much she admired his lovely wife. And he leaned down to ask, so seriously that Miss Jeffers couldn't believe she had heard what her reliable ears told her she had, "Did you know that Susan promised the minister she'd never leave me? She can't. Isn't that a wonderful thought?"

"Why, yes, I suppose so." Miss Jeffers was sure Susan had married a madman. Or at best a tyrant, or perhaps one of those murderous creatures they show on TV. "I'm sure she won't try," she said, hurrying on to look for Bitsy.

But Bitsy was not to be found. Guests were crowding into the dining room now, to watch Susan and Bobby cut their cake; and being small, Miss Jeffers couldn't see above all the heads. She wouldn't have found Bitsy had she brought a box to stand on, because Bitsy wasn't there.

Except for the few minutes when she had been walking down the aisle, trailing net and being watched by everyone, Bitsy had been in a fever of impatience to get on with her own affairs. She had spotted Keith in the back of the church and had managed to send him a small encouraging smile; and she had passed close to Davy, who was sitting between his mother and grandfather in the right front pew, and had given him a shy flick of her eyes. Then the two stars had taken over the pageant, and a dull time of waiting had begun for the rest of the cast. Bitsy had filled it by taking Susan's bouquet for her, giving it back, straightening Susan's train, and finally walking out behind her under the arch of sabers. Now she was free.

"Have you seen Keith?" she asked Parri, who

was standing alone in the living room, admiring her round bouquet of yellow roses.

"Uhhuh." Parri was deciding which bud she would save and press in her memory book, on the page next to the ring that Carlton Aiken had insisted she keep forever. "I just said how do you do to him, and he walked away. You don't think," she asked, her eyes brown globes of excitement, "that he went off to commit suicide, do you?"

"Don't be silly."

"Well, I'm sure *I* would—if I were a boy, that is. If any girl treated me the way Susan treated Keith and I treated Carlton, there'd be nothing for me to do but go off and kill myself. It's a frightful situation, and I don't see how Uncle Bobby can be so happy in the face of it."

Bitsy wanted to slap the silly child, but she went outside instead, and smiled at all the people who were eating creamed chicken patties and hot biscuits at the tables. There was no Keith sitting on the lacy bench. An engaged couple had it and were planning their own wedding. No Keith anywhere, and no Davy.

Men are selfish beasts, Bitsy thought, sauntering back aimlessly. Keith said we'd make plans for tonight just as soon as I was free, and Davy said we'd get the knot tied for Bobby and Susan and then have fun. But do they remember? Oh, no. They go off and do whatever they want to do.

She considered tasting the champagne punch, called a waiter to her, then waved him away.

It would look silly to stand alone, sipping punch by herself. Anne and Vance came out on the terrace, but they had Parri and Joshu with them, so she went up the steps as if she hadn't seen them, and covertly saw that they didn't so much as look her way. A fine wedding this was!

More people were coming outside now, and she smiled demurely as the men stepped back to make a little aisle for her to pass through on her way inside to the living room. Someone had brought a chair for Alcie, she noticed, and Gwenn was surrounded by a group of men who were too stupid to see that her made-up eyes were darting about in search of her movie-star husband; and Carrol, looking saintly, and Penny, looking countrified, were walking about, being helpful.

What a dull reception, Bitsy thought dejectedly, not realizing that it was only dull because her own plans had gone awry.

Then, presto chango, Keith magically appeared, produced like a rabbit out of a hat. She hadn't seen where he came from, but there he stood, holding two small white boxes filled with wedding cake. "These are for us to dream on," he said, giving her one. "It's supposed to bring you good luck."

"It's supposed to make you dream of the one you're going to marry," Bitsy corrected primly, laying her box on the piano beside her spray of deep golden chrysanthemums. "I don't see what good it will do you."

"Why not?" He looked straight at her and said,

"I've got as good a chance as the next guy. I'm not superstitious, but I'll take a crack at it for kicks. How about you?"

"I'm afraid to." Bitsy suddenly was. What if she should dream of Davy? Or even of little Joshu? She had no assurance that she would dream of Keith, clinging to her and pleading with her to save him. She felt committed to Keith. It was becoming almost traditional in the family that if one sister didn't take a man, the next one did. Look at Alcie and Susan. And even Peter. He was second choice with Tippy. "I don't think I'd want to know so long beforehand," she said crossly, pushing the little box farther under the flowers.

"Wouldn't you want to catch Susan's bridal bouquet?" he asked, wondering what had happened to his jolly little pal. "She and Bobby decided to throw it from the terrace, so they can stand together, you know. They're as happy as a couple of kids."

"Then I suppose I'd better go look after Daddy." Bitsy knew she sounded contrary when she only meant to sound helpful, so she added, "Poor Daddy. I'm all he has left, because you really can't count on boys. Neal has already gone and Vance will be going next year."

"The General's doing fine." Keith went right on wondering what had changed Bitsy. She had been beautiful in the wedding, prettier even than Susan; and although he had overheard Vance calling her "Mrs. Van Asterduster's plush horse" as he made a comical march along his family's receiving line, Keith hadn't thought she seemed bothered by it. "How about going outside and having some ice cream and cake," he suggested "so you'll be ready to catch Susan's bouquet? I want you to catch it, Doll."

"Well, if you say so." Bitsy's spirits lifted. If she couldn't comfort Keith she could make light chatter with him; and if that stupid Davy ever came out from wherever he was, he would see that she hadn't stood about waiting for him to suggest that the family stick together after Susan and Bobby left.

But he said, "Oh-oh, here they come. Hurry. Susan may be going to mingle again, or she may be going to throw the flowers. Let's get outside and be ready."

All of Susan's young friends and classmates had gathered below the stone railing of the terrace, and even Parri had squeezed through the crowd at the side door and ballooned down to be on the front row. Bitsy felt foolish as she lifted her long skirt and trailed daintily down the steps beside Keith. She would have stood far back but he pushed her forward; and when she looked up at Susan, she was sure Susan's smiling lips said, "Catch, honey."

Then Susan raised her arm and was given an unexpected assist by Bobby—just as his hand on top of hers had sent the saber slashing down through the wedding cake. A silver tray had been dented then, and now the bouquet flew straight up in the air before it plummeted down. Bitsy reached for it because both Keith and Susan wanted her to, but agile little Parri sprang high into space and snatched it.

"I got it!" Parri shrieked. "I got it!" And she began prancing in triumph.

"You can't have it!" Penny had somehow pushed through and was shaking Parri loose from a mass of white orchids. "I could murder you for this, Parrish MacDonald," she scolded, knowing that catching the bouquet, to Parri, was only comparable to being first off the high dive or reaching home base before another child could. "Honey, you'll have to give it back. Here." And she tossed the bouquet up to Susan. "Sorry," she called. "Let's do it again."

Bitsy caught it that time. She couldn't miss it, standing directly below the bride where Keith had put her, and with Parri's arms pinioned behind her. The orchids sailed high again but made a wider arc over the shrubbery, and all Bitsy had to do was to let them fall into her waiting hands. "Thank you, Susan," she said, embarrassed.

It had all gone according to custom now. The bride's younger sister had caught the bouquet. Bitsy saw Davy grinning at her from far back by the screen door, and she wanted to say to him exactly what Penny had said to Parri: "I could murder you!" But she smiled at Keith instead. They looked down on the flowers together before she gave them to him with a flirtatious little smile, and whispered, "Put these somewhere for me while I go help Susan." And she swept up the steps and past Davy as if he weren't there.

"Come in, darling," Susan said, stepping out of a puddle of white foam while she buttoned the blouse of her new navy-blue suit. "I've been wanting to remind you to help Ellin all you can tomorrow. The house will be a shambles, even with the caterers taking everything away and the boys putting the furniture back where it belongs. And don't let Alcie start off too early, and if Gwenn and Bill should come over to lunch . . ."

"Oh, I know what to do," Bitsy said crossly, stooping to pick up the wedding dress and feeling a run slide down her stocking. "I know how to run the house, Susan. I've done it, you know."

"Of course, I forgot." Susan was in her skirt now, and she stepped over the veil that was flowing from the bed to find her jacket. "I'm just nervous, I suppose. But it was a divine wedding, don't you think?"

"It was lovely." Bitsy looped the veil back out of the way, and listened to Bobby calling from the hall:

"Hey, Mrs. Parrish, are you ready? I am. *Mrs. Parrish?*"

"Coming." Susan rushed to the door and flung it open, and Bitsy turned away to move the veil from one bed to the other, then back again.

"Oh, darling," she could hear Bobby saying, with Susan pressed against him. "We're going away together. Alone. Oh, Daffy-dilly, Daffy-dilly! Just Susan Parrish and me, forever and ever."

Bitsy didn't watch them go down the stairway, she felt too suddenly sad. There would be no Susan to say, "Good morning, Bits." No Susan to make sure that the lamps were turned on in the evening, or to ask, "How did it go today, hon?" Bitsy felt sad and lonely, and she stood wiping away her tears until she remembered how happy Susan had looked, crushed in Bobby's arms.

"She's not dead, you silly girl," she told herself, following slowly. And she walked soberly out to the driveway where a crowd had gathered around Bobby's new car.

"The Parrishes are on their way," Bobby was saying, putting Susan tenderly inside, then turning to shout, "Buy all your cars from us so we won't starve to death. We thank you for your good wishes, but kindly remember Parrish Motors, Incorporated." Then he scowled and asked, "Who tied all that stuff on the car?"

Bitsy thought he was about to rip everything off: the JUST MARRIED placard, the old shoes and tin cans. But Susan opened her door so he hustled around to climb in and slam his. "Goodbye," he called. "My wife says we have to go, so we go."

Rice and rose petals rained down on the car. Rice struck it like hail, and rose petals drifted onto the sleeve of Susan's waving arm and clung there.

"Here, have some," Davy said, thrusting a cellophane bag of paper petals at Bitsy. "*Throw!*"

It was the first time she had seen him all afternoon; and here he was, commanding her to throw pieces of pink paper at a car that was already too far away to hit. "Why?" she asked, half-heartedly tossing a few that only drifted down at her feet.

"Because they're *married!*" Davy stood watching the car turn between the gateposts, grinning at the cheerful clanking and rattle it made. "Lang and I've been working on it ever since we got back from the church," he said proudly. "I found it stashed back of the garage, and we really dressed it." And then he turned to her and asked, as simply as if she hadn't been waiting for hours to hear it, "What shall we do tonight? We'd better get cracking."